D1087379

THE CASE OF THE
REVOLUTIONIST'S DAUGHTER:
SHERLOCK HOLMES
MEETS KARL MARX

THE CASE OF THE REVOLUTIONIST'S DAUGHTER: SHERLOCK HOLMES MEETS KARL MARX

BY

LEWIS S. FEUER

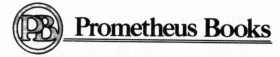

Prometheus Books

700 East Amherst St. Buffalo, New York 14215

Published in 1983 by
Prometheus Books
700 East Amherst Street
Buffalo, New York 14215

Printed in the United States of America

Library of Congress Card Catalog No. 83-61117
ISBN: 0-87975-245-9

To

Peter Worthington

. . . to fortitude I refer, in which I perceive courage and nobility.
Spinoza, *Ethics,* Part III,
Proposition LIX

Foreword

n the summer of 1926, having concluded my sopho-
more year at the City College of New York, I determined to spend my junior year as a student at the London School of Economics. I was prompted by several
reasons. I had become an ardent socialist, and was
reading in my spare time about the history of the socialist movement. I inquired of my professor of history, J. Salwyn Schapiro,
whether there was any scholar at an American university who had
made this subject his life work. He could think of none, but told me
that at the L.S.E. I would find a Professor Harold J. Laski, a
young man with a reputation for colossal erudition, but also an in-
fluential advisor to the foremost leaders of the British Labour
Party. I was at that time stirred by that political organization; its
story, from the beginning in 1906, when its twenty-nine elected
members entered the House of Commons wearing miners' caps as
their symbolic declaration, to their achievement in Parliament as
His Majesty's Opposition, confirmed an enthusiasm for what the
Fabian socialists called "the inevitability of gradualness." The
British general strike that very year, moreover, had made me feel
that the working classes were now in genuine motion to achieve the
socialist society. Who knows, I wondered, but perhaps in Britain I
might witness the dream of John Ball, the fourteenth-century
Lollard agitator for an equal society, realized through the courage
and initiative of the British working-class movement. I would be at
hand to chronicle the pending great days, to record in Gibbonesque

prose the decline and fall of the British capitalist system.

With the help of a subsidy from a Canadian uncle and a letter of introduction to Professor Laski, I sailed for Britain on the old ship *Berengaria*. Soon afterward, I awaited Professor Laski at his office. In all candor, I must acknowledge that he was not the imposing person I had pictured in my imagination. He was small, slight, almost frail, and his black-rimmed glasses set against his pale skin gave him the appearance of a convalescent. He spoke as if he were addressing an audience and, marvelously, his words issued as if they had been prepared from a carefully edited manuscript, except that they were indeed his spontaneous utterances. He welcomed me into the company of political scientists, asked after several professors at the City College, and inquired minutely into the state of socialism in New York City. He was also much concerned with the case of Sacco and Vanzetti, which was then being argued with growing intensity, both in the United States and Europe. Sacco and Vanzetti were two Italian anarchists who had been convicted for murdering a man during an alleged banditry near Boston in 1920. Professor Laski spoke warmly of the efforts of his friend Professor Felix Frankfurter, of the Harvard Law School, to plead the case for the two Italian peddlers before the American conscience. At that point he remarked that, if only Sherlock Holmes were alive to investigate the facts, the Italians would shortly be exonerated, and the prejudice of the Brahman Yankee Protestant court fully exposed. This led us to compare notes on Sherlock Holmes. We found we shared a common admiration, whereupon Professor Laski invited me to attend the regular monthly meeting of the L.S.E.'s branch of the Baker Street Irregulars. I became a faithful attendant, and a few months later enjoyed immensely his paper on "The Politics of Sherlock Holmes"; by contrast, his lectures on political pluralism in his course on political philosophy belabored the commonplace truth that the existence of independent associations such as churches, unions, and corporations limits the power of government, and prevents it from becoming tyrannical. But perhaps political philosophies become dangerous when they cease to be commonplace.

Several of the thirty or so Irregulars raised the interesting question: Could Professor Laski, author of the volume *Communism* and an editor of the *Communist Manifesto,* throw any light on the question of whether Sherlock Holmes had ever met Marx and Engels? Laski replied cautiously that the extant writings of Dr. Watson left the matter indeterminate, though Watson's agent, Arthur Conan Doyle, had from time to time evinced a sympathetic interest in socialism. I noticed that one elderly Irregular, very distinguished looking with his gray hair and mustache, listened most intently to the professor's remarks. Then Laski, in his precise parliamentary manner, the fingers of both hands balanced in his left and right vest-pockets, launched into a powerful critique of the Soviet Union: As Irregulars, he said, we should take special umbrage against the attacks on Sherlock Holmes and other detective memoirs that were appearing regularly in the Soviet press, especially in the *Literaturnaya Gazeta.* The communist critics, it seemed, regarded the detective in bourgeois society as an enemy of the proletariat; moreover, they noted, it was a matter of record that Holmes had assisted the Czarist government in the matter of the shooting of General Trepov. To which Laski replied that the great detective had above all been an agent against all forms of human exploitation wherein some evil individuals used others as means only, and that his sympathies for the Russian populist revolutionaries, known as the Nihilists, had been shown unequivocally in the case of Mme. Anna, the Nihilist, in *The Adventure of the Golden Pince-Nez.*

At this observation, the elderly Irregular exclaimed audibly: "Hear! Hear!" As the meeting adjourned, he approached Laski, whom I was congratulating and thanking for his illuminating address, and asked whether he could call at the professor's office at the L.S.E.; he wished to bring some information that would answer the question as to whether Sherlock Holmes had known Dr. Karl Marx. The elderly gentleman was so distinguished in his bearing, still almost erect in a military fashion, despite his advanced years, that there could be no question in Professor Laski's mind about seeing him. He asked the gentleman whether three o'clock the next afternoon would be convenient for him. "Excellent!" said our fellow Irregular, and bowing, he turned to leave.

"Might I ask," said Professor Laski, "what is your name?"

"Dr. John H. Watson," said the elderly gentleman, as he

proceeded to the door.

Laski and I looked at each other with amazement.

"Can it be," asked Laski, "that Dr. Watson is still alive and evidently well, or is this fine-looking gentleman an impostor or a madman?"

"He certainly looks," I said, "as I would have imagined Dr. Watson to be if he had lived into advanced years."

Professor Laski regarded me and said emphatically: "You must be present tomorrow afternoon when I meet our purported Dr. Watson. Perhaps I shall need a witness for a case of identity. Or better still we may learn such unusual information that I should like to have another scholar, another recorder, present with me for the documentation."

The following day I was at Professor Laski's office well before the appointed hour, much excited by the pending discussion with Dr. John H. Watson. Even Professor Laski's pale face was slightly aglow with dramatic tension. Precisely on the hour Dr. Watson came walking slowly but erectly down the corridor; he carried in his right hand a parcel. The professor greeted him effusively, and introduced me as a scholar in political theory and Holmeseana. Dr. Watson took the offered upholstered seat, then muttered: "The chairs that William Morris designed were much better." He complimented Professor Laski on the portraits of Marx and Engels that adorned the office walls. "Those are excellent replications of their features, but in those days people acted parts when they sat for photographs. Dr. Marx, when I met him, had none of that fierce, leonine expression, and Mr. Engels, for all his magisterial bearing, conveyed the sense of a man who realizes he is an outsider."

"Then, Dr. Watson, you knew both Marx and Engels!" exclaimed Professor Laski with amazement.

"That I did," responded Dr. Watson, "and it was forty-four years ago that Mr. Engels came to consult Sherlock Holmes."

"Then why have you not written about it? Why have you concealed it? This would be a scoop in historical antiquarianism that would put the Piltdown Man to scorn."

"I was never concerned with 'scoops,' Professor Laski, to use your odd phrase. Not even when I wrote regularly for The Strand was I concerned with either sensationalism, or the bizarre, or newspaper headlines. I think I wrote for the same reason that Socrates' friends wrote about him: Sherlock Holmes was a man of intellectual powers and physical strength who stood for certain simple ideas that are going out of fashion—honor, courage, loyalty, the respect for human dignity. Other men have immersed themselves in the goods of life; Holmes took the harder task, of seeking out the men of evil in order to thwart and undo them, yet he never allowed their evil to infiltrate his soul."

"I do indeed accept your rebuke," said Professor Laski. "My good friend Justice Oliver Wendell Holmes, Jr., shares your philosophy exactly, and in the letters we have been exchanging for several years he has expounded his soldier's faith, and repudiated my socialist modernism. Justice Holmes was a veteran as yourself, Dr. Watson, and was wounded and near death several times during the American Civil War."

"True, Professor Laski, war in the nineteenth century, for all its bloodshed, heightened the sense of gallantry. Not so in the twentieth, where its aftermath is cynicism, mockery, selfishness. Sometimes I fear that we lost our best young men in the last war and that henceforth we will be a land without heroes. But I really must come to the purpose of my visit, Professor Laski, and not take up your time unnecessarily.

"Many years ago, in 1881, personal problems arose in the life of Dr. Karl Marx and his family which led to a call for the services of my friend Mr. Sherlock Holmes. In the course of Holmes's investigations, I accompanied him in his forays into the world of Bohemian socialist 'intellectuals,' as they are now described. I found it more exotic than the Afghan villages I had known. It was the most political case in which Holmes was ever involved, the most delicate, from a personal standpoint, and it required his utmost discretion and tact. Afterward, its characters went their own, perhaps inevitable, routes to unhappiness. But before the case was terminated, it brought Holmes the deepest personal loss of his life and ignited in him the long years' duel against the perpetrator of that crime.

"I could not publish my account of these events so long as any of Dr. Marx's children were alive. Then, the later rise of the European socialist parties and the Bolshevik Revolution made me reluctant to involve Holmes's name in political acrimony; he himself did not wish the facts of his personal unhappiness brought to public view. However, now that the political atmosphere is calmer, and I am very old, I wish, Professor Laski, to make you the trustee of this narrative. When you deem it prudent and timely to publish this history, you may do so. I shall have all the necessary legal documents prepared. I am asking you therefore whether you would accept custodianship and responsibility for this particular work of mine."

With alacrity and enthusiasm, Professor Harold J. Laski accepted the guardianship of the unpublished Holmes-Marx history. He remarked to Dr. Watson, however, that in view of the importance of the document he wished to have a photographic copy made that he would entrust to me. Then, if any mishap should befall him or the document, a copy would still remain in my American hands, with the authority to publish. Dr. Watson agreed to these amendments, and informed the professor that his solicitors would soon conclude the negotiations with him.

It is needless to set forth the later details of negotiation. They ended happily and, in the last years of Dr. Watson's life, Laski's generous visits to his Cornwall cottage were a source of joy to him. The recurrent political crises, however, as well as Laski's own evolution toward Marxism, led him to keep postponing the publication of the Holmes-Marx story. Professor Laski came to dislike the thought of any publication in which Marx did not fill the stage as an intellectual and spiritual giant. He did, however, entrust a third copy to the famed Menshevik scholar Boris Nicolaevsky, keeper of the Social Democratic archives, and was most distressed when it was stolen in a burglary executed by agents of the Soviet secret police. Then the war intervened; Laski's copy was destroyed when his library was burnt during the Nazi bombardment of London. Toward the end of his life, Laski, disillusioned by Soviet actions during 1948 to 1950 in Berlin and Czechoslovakia, was thinking of allowing my copy of the manuscript to be published. His premature death terminated this intention. A codicil in his will, however, still admonished me not to publish the story until the 1980s. As Laski put it: "It would make good reading as 1984 approaches."

The Case of the
Revolutionist's Daughter:
Sherlock Holmes Meets Karl Marx

t was the cold wintry month of December 1881, made all the colder in my heart by the recent death of my wife, Mary Morstan Watson. Sherlock Holmes, with all his generosity, had invited me back to the old rooms I shared with him at No. 221B Baker Street. He seemed to have kept my room unused since I had left, as if he would have been intruding on my shade had he converted it to some practical purpose. I gazed intently at the fire, thinking of the transitoriness of things, and the truth of the homely wisdom that sees in the flickering flame the eternal symbol of the human life. I wondered whether there could really be communication with the spirits of the beyond, and recalled how five years earlier, in 1876, the spiritualist medium Henry Slade had been prosecuted as a common fraud by the doughty young scientist, Edwin Ray Lankester.

Suddenly I heard my friend's voice say in comforting tones: "There is no answer to those questions, Watson. We shall never know so long as we inhabit this earth."

"But my dear Holmes, how did you know what I was thinking?"

"What else could you have been thinking of, Watson, after your bereavement? But take comfort, my good fellow. Your memoir *The Sign of Four* will be an abiding memorial to your

13

wife's beauty and grace. I do acknowledge that when it appeared I was displeased by its account of the science of deduction, but that is of little importance now.''

"I do protest Holmes. I am a man of science. Indeed, while I was attending lectures on medicine at the university, I took a course on the principles of science with the brilliant logician Professor Jevons. I never have heard so luminous a lecturer; he demonstrated

HOLMES WAS WARMING
TO THE ARGUMENT.

to us how our principles of reasoning could be translated into mathematical symbols."

"My dear Watson, that is precisely where I differ from you. At college I too did some reading on the science of deduction. Let me assure you, Watson, that one of the masters there, William Whewell, proved that John Stuart Mill forgot that no train of reasoning, no series of observations, will get anywhere unless they are guided by a hypothesis."

"I disagree with you, Holmes; we begin with facts, with observations, and having anticipations—hypotheses—serves only to bias what we see. Charles Darwin, my dear Holmes, said he was a follower of Bacon."

Sherlock Holmes was warming to the argument and thrusting at the fire, as if preparing some statement of conclusive weight. Suddenly there was a firm knock on our door; then it was repeated.

"This is a man who didn't stop to be announced by Mrs. Hudson," said Holmes as he arose and opened the door.

At the threshold stood a sturdy, well-built man of more than average height, with a full, well-kempt gray-streaked beard, evidently in his late fifties, or early sixties.

"May I come in, gentlemen?" he queried most courteously, with an almost formal bow. There was a slight German accent to his carefully pronounced words.

"By all means, sir," said Holmes as he beckoned our visitor to a newly acquired chair.

Our visitor, after glancing about the room, to our amazement examined the chair's design carefully, even noting its almost hidden number and signature. "Made at Kelmscott, I see," he said, "by my good friend Mr. William Morris. I like his chairs more than his theories, as I have often told him."

"You came to England then, I presume," said Holmes, "after the revolutionary party failed in 1848 to bring democracy to Germany. And you were one of those who took up arms for the revolution."

Our visitor looked at Holmes with odd surprise.

"I have never thought that English empiricism could think with such deductive power as our German dialectics, but you, Mr. Holmes, astonish me. How did you know?"

"Very simple, my dear sir. On your coat's lapel you still wear the red insignia of the revolutionists. Your speech is excellent, and your accent so slight that obviously you have enjoyed our English liberties for many years. You know the anarchist theories of William Morris well enough to reject them, which indicates that, though a revolutionist yourself, you favor the side with more discipline and order. Your eye, as you glanced around, paused approvingly to note the rifle on our wall. All of which suggests a man with military experience."

Our visitor laughed good-heartedly. "Yes," he said. "My friends still call me 'the General,' and, indeed, I fought for our revolution at Baden during its last glorious days, until we had to retreat and flee for our lives."

"I feel honored, sir," said Holmes, "to welcome to my chambers a veteran of a noble-hearted revolution. Would your side had won."

I regarded Holmes with astonished interest, for I had never known him to take any interest in political matters or to express political views. This sudden declaration of sympathy for the German revolutionary party came to me as a surprise.

"My dear Holmes," I said, "I never knew you were an expert on revolution as well as on crime."

"Come, my dear Watson, I know no more than an average reader of the *Times* who has on idle days listened at Hyde Park to enthusiastic preachers of revolution expounding their philosophies. I find their ideas on crime based on singularly little knowledge and even less judgment of men's characters."

Our visitor turned to me. "I am grateful to you, Dr. Watson, for the great pleasure I derived from my reading of your account in *A Study in Scarlet*. For from you I learned that Mr. Holmes brings to bear a disinterested judgment on matters connected with the German revolutionary party."

"Sir," I replied, "I feel flattered indeed that my literary effort should have given you some pleasant moments, but none of the characters in that episode could be described as revolutionaries."

Our visitor laughed. "Not at all," he said. "But your story did narrate how Mr. Holmes refused to be deceived by that word 'Rache,' scrawled in blood across the wall of the room where the murdered man lay. It was meant to mislead the police by suggesting that this murder was an act of revenge on the part of a German revolutionary secret society. Mr. Holmes saw through the chicanery at once. And your *Sign of Four* is indeed a story of the after-days of greedy imperialist men who plundered India and wrought an empire. My friend Karl Marx has written about that.''

Holmes, in his easy chair, bowed his head. "Thank you, Mr. Engels," he said quietly. "You are most kind in your judgment. But what, might I ask, brings one of the two most revered revolutionists in the world to my sitting room?''

"Then you have known all along that I am Friedrich Engels?''

"Who but Friedrich Engels, sir, could refer in such terms of intimacy and equality to 'my friend Karl Marx'? I did indeed study your writings three years ago. Our government briefly retained me following the two attempts to assassinate the German emperor. Scotland Yard was fearful that an international terrorist movement was in the making, and I spent a week at the British Museum reading your interesting works. May I compliment you and your collaborator on the stirring prose of the *Communist Manifesto*?''

Mr. Engels looked very gratified, as does every author who meets an appreciative reader. Then his face became serious.

"I am here, Mr. Holmes, on a matter of the greatest delicacy. It concerns the family of Karl Marx himself. A public scandal would destroy the remaining years of Marx and his wife and bring shame and bewilderment to the world's socialist movement. I know I can trust you, Mr. Holmes, where tact and consideration are required. I have heard from Irene Adler with what circumspection you intervened on behalf of that pathetic incompetent prince of Central Europe.''

Holmes was staggered for a moment. He had not as yet given me permission to publish the details of *A Scandal in Bohemia,* indeed, in part, out of the warm regard he had for "the Woman," Irene Adler.* He had evidently heard nothing about her since that case was resolved to the satisfaction of the King of Bohemia; now,

---

*It must be acknowledged that when I published *A Scandal in Bohemia,* I used certain devices to conceal the identity of the chief character. I placed the story in 1888, whereas the events actually took place in 1881; there was no hereditary king of Bohemia, but a dynasty still ruled in the Austro-Hungarian Empire.

18

through the intermediary of the coauthor of the *Communist Manifesto,* came word of her own reciprocated regard.

"Might I inquire, Mr. Engels," said Holmes, "how you happen to have heard these kind judgments from Miss Irene Adler?"

"Very simple, Mr. Holmes. The comradeship of the international socialist movement is a close and confiding one. Miss Adler is the cousin of the most talented young socialist in Europe, the future chief, I hope, of the Austrian party, Dr. Victor Adler. He is a man much like Irene, brilliant, charming, courteous, and with an insight into human character that has made him Vienna's most promising young doctor of nervous illnesses. But he feels the calling to work for our movement. The workers adore and trust him; in fact, everybody does, including old Emperor Francis Joseph himself. When Victor Adler speaks in the Viennese parliament, his wit will make even the opposition become historical materialists, at least for the duration of his address. Irene has visited my house several times for my evenings-at-home, and entertains us with her singing. She told me about you and recommended you most highly to aid me in the present problem."

I sat there bewildered. Frederick Engels spoke with the authority and assurance of a personified historical force. I knew nothing of this historical force, whether indeed it existed or was mainly born of an overheated imagination; and, if it did exist, I doubted that I should approve of it. My family in the last elections had stanchly supported Disraeli and his Conservative Party; though Disraeli was a Jew, he was devoted to the empire, and we soldiers of the Afghan campaigns appreciated that. I had never heard of Dr. Victor Adler, and to speak with candor, I had a distaste for doctors who treated "nervous illnesses." Perhaps as a former army surgeon, I thought of wounds, injuries, and physical pains as our province and would prefer to leave mental philosophy to clergymen. I had never heard Engels's term "historical materialists"; what could they be? Were they perhaps spiritualists who believed they could materialize the appropriate person at the time he was needed? I forebore asking any question and sat in silent fascination with this unusual man. I noticed moreover that I could not bring myself to speak of Engels as "Friedrich" but only as "Frederick." My insular, homespun British ways found something harsh and repellent in the German words and address.

"Miss Irene Adler has my unstinted admiration," said Holmes. "May we now proceed to hear of the occurrences that have affected the family of Mr. Marx. I assure you that my colleague and I will receive your account with the utmost confidence."

Engels drew himself up.

"My friend Karl Marx is the father of three daughters. The two older ones live in France, where they are married to French socialists, and are reasonably well off. The third daughter, Eleanor, is Marx's favorite. To look at her is to be reminded of Marx in his youth—her eyes alert and poetic, her spirit ardent and self-sacrificing, her intelligence extraordinary. He calls her 'Tussy,' and he says 'Tussy is I.' She is the son he would have wanted. She goes among the gas workers to agitate and help them organize their union; she joined with William Morris in the Social Democratic Federation, and she writes for our socialist papers. She reads, studies, and translates the books of French novelists. Her father used to frequent the library of the British Museum almost every day; there he sat with his books and notes composing his great work, *Das Kapital.* Have you read it, Mr. Holmes?"

Holmes shook his head. He was listening, enthralled by Engels's description of a political underworld that was almost as unfamiliar to him as to myself.

"Ah, Mr. Holmes," continued Engels, *"Das Kapital* is like a symphony by Beethoven. It gathers together the events of history and gives them a theme, a direction, and an ending that is an ode to joy. It is the poem of the suffering and redemption of the despised lower classes, and it forecasts their triumph; but it is also a work of science, more reasoned and more documented than even the Herbert Spencer of whom your countrymen are so proud."

Holmes moved a bit restlessly. He had listened patiently to Engels's digression upon Karl Marx's book; he always tried to master for himself the details of the background against which the actors in his cases moved, almost like a stage director who realizes the value of precise stage directions. Yet Holmes himself obviously disliked hearing our German visitor affirming the superiority of German thinkers over British ones.

"I recognize," said Holmes, "the signal importance of

Mr. Karl Marx as the guiding chieftan of the International Workingmen's Association. I even recall that the *Times* reported during the civil strife of the Paris Commune that its atrocities and the execution of hostages were the work of Marx's followers, acting in accordance with his precepts. All that however is a decade past, and surely you are brought here by something more immediate."

I must acknowledge that Mr. Engels seemed to me to have nothing of the revolutionist about him. He seemed to like to talk on like a university lecturer grown accustomed to an audience of undergraduates who were held to attention by the constraints of rules. One could scarcely imagine him coping with the attention of a group of free British workingmen hurling questions, interruptions, sarcasms, jeers, and even eggs at the speaker. He resumed, however, his discourse.

"Now, Mr. Holmes, I was telling you of Marx's youngest daughter, Eleanor. When her father had to stop haunting the British Museum, Eleanor took his place. She sat there translating the novel about the bourgeois family, Madame ———. I forgot the name, but it's by a French novelist Flaubert. She also did the plays of this Norwegian, Ibsen, that all the young are talking about. But, unfortunately, Mr. Holmes, Eleanor's ambitions didn't stop with translating plays; she wanted to act in them, to play Nora as she ran away from her husband, from her doll's house, to live in liberated love. This was more than her father could stand. Between ourselves, Mr. Holmes, Marx might have talked theoretically about free love when he was young, but he scarcely even practiced it then. And, when his daughters grew up, he watched over them like a eunuch guarding a sultan's harem. No bourgeois father inspected his daughters' suitors more closely than Marx. And he warned a couple of them who burned too ardently to mend their ways or be barred from the Marx household. And to see his dear Tussy mixing with a Bohemian crowd was an agony to the Moor—"

Holmes interrupted. "You call Marx 'the Moor'?"

Engels laughed good-naturedly: "Marx is so swarthy that we have long called him 'the Moor'."

"I thought for a moment that possibly it was a reference to the famed jealousy of Othello, the Moor of Venice," Holmes remarked.

"Maybe you're not entirely wrong. For as far as jealousy is concerned, Marx looks on Eleanor's friends with a jealousy just this side of incest. I teased him about this when we discussed Lewis Morgan's theories of the origins of the family. At any rate, Marx pleaded with his daughter not to try to become an actress. But Tussy modeled herself on Ellen Terry, took classes in acting, and acted and read for small theatrical parties. The toll she paid for her way of life was high. She began to stop eating, almost starved, then collapsed. Marx and his wife pleaded with Tussy to confide in them, to trust them, to no avail. He looked for a doctor who might watch over his spirit-sick child. Marx had met a brilliant young scientist, a friend of Darwin, one in whom he could rest his confidence, Edwin Ray Lankester, of the University of London."

"You mean the same man who prosecuted the medium Slade for willful fraud?"

"The very same man, the intimate associate of Huxley as well as Darwin; in fact, he's regarded as their presumptive intellectual heir."

"That was wise of Dr. Marx—choosing a physician for his knowledge and character rather than for his politics," Holmes interposed.

"Not quite, Mr. Holmes. Lankester is not a physician. But he brought with him a Dr. Horace Donkin, who began to treat Tussy."

"Dr. Donkin, his collaborator in prosecuting Slade?" asked Holmes.

"Yes, an anti-spiritualist, and a fine doctor. He diagnosed Tussy's illness as a kind of despairing withdrawal from life."

"I am not a consulting physician," said Holmes, "but a consulting detective. I assume something has since happened that warrants my services."

"Yes," replied Engels. "Tussy has disappeared."

Holmes regarded Engels impassively. "Did she leave no letter?"

"None whatsoever."

"Did any friend of hers convey a message?"

"None at all. She just vanished."

"When did this take place?"

"Just three and a half weeks ago. Marx and his wife have been out of their minds with grief and worry."

"Had anything happened of an unusual character immediately before her vanishing?"

"Nothing unusual. She seemed during the preceding month or two to have been in a more cheerful mood than usual, and stayed out in the evenings more often. There was a long argument one evening between them about agnosticism, freethought, and religion."

"Really. Might I know how it arose?"

"Tussy said one day that she had met some of the writers of *The National Reformer*. That journal, as perhaps you may not know, is published by Charles Bradlaugh and his freethinkers. I look at it every once in a while. It publishes excellent articles about Darwin's work on evolution, but on all questions of philosophy and politics, it is utterly petty bourgeois—philosophy from the commercial shopkeeper's standpoint. Anyhow, Marx told Tussy that Bradlaugh, the 'Atheist Tribune,' was a vainglorious man who postured about atheism but had no constructive ideas. Also, Marx told Tussy that Bradlaugh had had the effrontery to charge in print that Marx was probably a paid police spy working for Bismarck. The Moor was annoyed that Tussy still liked to attend the Sunday services of Bradlaugh's Secular Society. He once told her and her mother that that was no place for them, and he said repeatedly that if Tussy had religious longings, she would do better to read the Jewish prophets. He himself was once taken with them, and had attended Bruno Bauer's lectures on Isaiah. That is a stage of development we all go through. But Charles Bradlaugh is a silly schoolboy fancying himself brave because he throws bricks at a God that does not exist. Why doesn't he fight real enemies like the bourgeois props to capitalism? The man once had the gall to try to join the International Workingmen's Association to try to make converts for 'Freethought.' The Executive Council had the good sense to send him packing. It was fighting the capitalist order, bringing help to striking workers, exposing the secret police and the anarchist criminals alike; the International had no time to waste on pamphlets against the Book of Genesis. They could leave that to Huxley and his lectures to workingmen. Bradlaugh thinks that he is a hero

---

of history of Carlylean proportions because he got himself admitted to Parliament without taking the religious oath; now he glories in his atheism. I'd rather have a Byron communing with the Devil himself but speaking up for the workers, and that, the atheist actor Bradlaugh will never do.''

I had never seen Holmes listen so intently to such a long, rambling political monologue; Engels's acerbic comments seemed to me to have the overtones of the crank or crackpot insisting that he was a kind of favored prophet of history. I had never heard of him, nor did I know of a single book or article by him. Yet he talked as if he had the authority to deny Spencer, Mill, Bradlaugh, and all those in the forefront of British thought. Holmes, however, taut with attention, responded.

"Mr. Engels, I am most indebted to you for explicating to me your political philosophy. Many persons flee from home because of personal cruelties or indignities, or because they feel the call to make a fortune in some novel industry or backward land. Miss Eleanor Marx is obviously not one of those. Her father has evidently cherished her, and her mother is a gentle woman. Young women are, however, persuaded to escape their homes mainly by lovers. If Eleanor Marx has left home, it was most probably not because of the blandishments of wealth or social position. Only one kind of person could have achieved a dominance over Eleanor Marx's emotions—a man whose powers of intellect and dedication to the Cause would have seemed to her every whit as great if not greater than those of her father. But this person, I fear, might also possess an admixture of egotism, a readiness to accept the self-sacrifice of others to his own indulgence. In all likelihood, therefore, we should find Eleanor Marx lost somewhere among political philosophers. That is why I have listened to your account with much interest.''

"Did you ever at college attend lectures on political philosophy, Mr. Holmes?'' asked Engels, who scrutinized Holmes closely, as if discerning a fellow philosopher.

Holmes laughed, "No. The lectures which I heard were mainly on chemistry, anatomy, and criminal law. Frederick Pollock used to sprinkle his law lectures with some philosophy of a highly metaphysical kind and quote the sayings of a Dutch-Jewish mystic. But I never had a taste for that sort of thing and am content to leave the unknowable to itself. There was no John Ruskin at my university to urge the youth to build an empire, or at least a country road, nor any Green or Toynbee to stir young men to go among the poor and found what they now call 'settlement houses.' "

Our distinguished revolutionary politician seemed pleased that no social idealism had ever possessed Sherlock Holmes.

"Then our dealings can be straightforwardly commercial," he said. "No nexus of comradeship, but a plain cash nexus. I have high confidence, Mr. Holmes, that you will not only find Tussy, but will bring her home to the Moor. I shall pay you well, for as Marx would say, your labor-power is highly skilled. In return, I shall expect the utmost discretion. For if Marx's enemies pick up any rumors they will hasten to write their scandal-mongering articles in their parasite papers; I can see their large titles—'Marx's Daughter Deserts Father,'; 'The Dictator of the International Can't Dictate to his Daughter,'; 'Revolutionist Daughter Rebels Against Ex-Revolutionary Marx.' There would be innuendoes and insinuations to which it would be impossible to reply. If Marx were younger, he'd challenge such people to duels for their calumnies. Marx, you may not know, believes that duels are thoroughly justified in matters of honor. But he is too old now to wield a saber and, in any case, English law doesn't allow it. So I shall look forward to the restraints of your silence, Mr. Holmes."

"My fee, Mr. Engels, will be no more than customary. This case, I hope, will not be too different from the usual ones of a daughter deserting her family's home, though the extraordinary political background introduces features I have never previously encountered. Might I, however, Mr. Engels, have the pleasure of a short meeting with Dr. Karl Marx? There are a few questions I should like to ask, and he might wish to ask me some himself."

"I shall advise him to see you, Mr. Holmes, though I trust you will bear in mind that he is much distraught. Would tomorrow morning at ten o'clock be convenient for you? Here is Marx's card; he lives at 41 Maitland Park, Haverstock Hill. I have much enjoyed meeting you, Mr. Holmes. Would it had been for a less melancholy purpose."

Mr. Frederick Engels bowed to us both courteously; Holmes opened the door, and escorted him down the stairway and to the street. Through the window, I watched Engels quickly hail a hansom cab and climb in energetically as it sped away.

When Holmes returned, he took his recently purchased pipe from the mantelpiece, and then, opening a tin of Beaconfield tobacco, filled his pipe with its leaves. A curiously Oriental flavor soon filled the sitting room. Holmes reclined in his favorite reading chair. He pointed to the tobacco tin that was adorned with the picture of the recently deceased former Prime Minister Mr. Benjamin Disraeli, later Earl of Beaconsfield.

HOLMES RECLINED IN HIS FAVORITE CHAIR.

"Do you know, Watson, there were never two men more different than those two Jews, Disraeli and Marx? The one, joining himself with the empire and the old established classes and religion, a preserver in every sense, the other, intent on shattering the society that shelters him, instituting the rule of the machine-tenders, demolishing the religious institutions—a destroyer in every sense. Yet Britain enabled them both to pursue their missions."

"I have never myself found Disraeli's novels real or interesting, Holmes," I replied. "His characters are foppish; I prefer the manly deportment of Walter Scott's heroes. Still I always felt that as prime minister he defined Britain's imperial purpose. In the hospital at Lahore, one day, the senior nurse read to us Disraeli's speech on the Afghan War, and the role of England in leading the Indian races and keeping at bay the Russian Cossacks; we were all stirred, and stood silent. The Jew could speak for us, and I, for one, admired his frankness in saying 'race is all.' Meanwhile, Holmes, I fear you have a grave case on your hands. The poor girl Eleanor Marx may have come to grief; I dread to think of her wandering alone in London, too guilty and ashamed to return home."

"I don't think it has come to that, Watson. But tomorrow we

shall meet her famous father and be the better able to judge." He reached for a volume in his collection of books on crime and criminals. "I shall drift off to sleep reading this small book, *The Secret History of the International Workingmen's Association.* I bought it a couple of years ago, but only perused it. Its anarchist author had some uncomplimentary things to say about the dictatorial Karl Marx and his aide-de-camp Friedrich Engels. Mr. Marx, on the other hand, seems to have regarded its author as an unprincipled brigand, ready to commit any crime for the alleged sake of the social revolution, and sanctifying bombs, poison, and daggers with the formula that a humane end justifies inhuman means. Tomorrow we shall begin to explore political evil. Good night, Watson."

"A good rest, Holmes."

Chapter Two

he next day Holmes was up early and breakfasting lightly on eggs, telling Mrs. Hudson that he would have no bacon or potatoes. After studying the newspapers, he observed laconically that the "agony columns" contained no message either to or from Eleanor Marx. Soon we were on our way to Maitland Park Road. When I protested weakly that Karl Marx might prefer to see him alone, Holmes replied: "When dealing with makers of history, a historian should be there. It gives the history-maker the audience he craves, and also guarantees that the narrative will not be his prerogative."

"Machiavelli," I responded, "could not have said it better."

As our hansom cab climbed Haverstock Hill, Holmes and I admired the calm dignity of the neighborhood. We looked curiously at Marx's house as our cab left us. It was a

HOLMES WAS UP EARLY AND BREAKFASTING LIGHTLY ON EGGS.

fine-looking three-story house, with three granite pillars at the entrace and a base of large marble blocks. Each upper story had three large, well-designed windows. Some thick bushes and a tree, leafless in the winter, filled a small garden alongside the first story.

"Scarcely the house in which I'd expect the world's premier revolutionist to be found," I could not help remarking.

"Precisely the house, my dear Watson, which a father would like to provide for his three daughters approaching the age when suitors call."

Holmes rang the bell. A short, stocky, aged housemaid answered, and with a heavy German accent bade us follow her to the second story: "Mr. Marx is waiting for you."

We were ushered into a room that was obviously Marx's study. Every wall was fortified with ceiling-high bookcases, stacked with volumes of all shapes, sizes, and colors, papers, journals, manuscripts, and boxes. In the middle stood a large desk and lamp, and standing in front to greet us, Mr. Karl Marx himself. He was of medium height but looked taller as he stood firmly with his broad shoulders thrust back; his shaggy gray beard and a thick mane of hair gave him a lionlike expression. His German-tinged speech had a gracious quality as he shook hands with us and, with a sad touch to his voice, told us we were welcome and bade us to be seated in two large oversoft chairs. He said he was pleased that I had accompanied Mr. Holmes, as the advice of a physician might be helpful in finding his Tussy.

Holmes began by saying that he had a fairly good idea of Eleanor's interests and ambitions, but he added that he knew nothing of her friends and associations. "Could you, Mr. Marx, tell us who her friends are, what interests they share, and where they have met?"

Karl Marx thought for a few moments. Then he said, "Of late, Tussy has taken to spending more of her time at the British Museum Library. It seems a whole group of young English men and women who are drawn to socialism spend their time there. She met a Beatrice Potter, who it appears is a great friend of your philosopher, Spencer. Miss Potter is studying the life of the London poor; she is what you Englishmen call a 'sociologist'; that is, she studies social facts without a rational theory. Then there's a young Irishman who alternates all day between writing novels and reading the French translation of my book *Das Kapital*. I can't remember his name. Tussy has also gotten to know a fine young American scholar, a student of Greek art, who lectures at King's College; his name is Charles Waldstein, but I don't know how well acquainted they are. He has been to visit me a number of times. Tussy also has been friends with a woman from South Africa, Olive Schreiner, high-strung and hysterical; she's writing a novel too. I think Tussy has also talked with a poet Thomson, James Thomson, who has translated Heine—"

"Do you mean the Thomson who wrote *The City of Dreadful Night*?" interrupted Holmes, who was jotting down in his small notebook the names that Marx had mentioned.

"The same man," replied Marx.

"A poem of unmitigated pessimism as to the human lot," said Holmes, "and leaving open only the escape through suicide."

Marx's face was shadowed. "Of one thing I am certain," he said, "Tussy is alive. She would never kill herself. She becomes depressed, she is willful, and she is stubborn. But she will not kill herself. She has grown up with me, listening to my stories every night before bed, long adventure stories. She has courage and faith in life; she has faith in our movement. No, she will not kill herself."

A side door opened and a wan, elderly woman stood at the threshold. Her features still looked distinguished, for the lines of an enduring nobility had replaced her earlier beauty. She was supported by the housemaid who had welcomed us. Marx jumped to his feet. Holmes and I both rose. Marx said: "May I present my wife, Madame Jenny von Westphalen Marx?"

We bowed to her. "I trust that we have not been disturbing you with our words, Mrs. Marx," said Holmes.

Mrs. Marx looked at him wistfully, almost in appeal. There was a searching look of desperation in her face. "Oh, Mr. Holmes," she said, in a tone that was like melancholy music from a Schumann concerto. "You must find my poor daughter. She is tired, and she is sick. We have demanded too much of her; we have placed on her burdens that no child should be asked to carry. She is self-giving and idealistic; she does not know the harsh realities of life to which we can only submit. You will find our Tussy and tell her that we love her."

Karl Marx grew pale as his wife spoke. He waved his hand once or twice as if he meant her to stop speaking but did not know how to effect it. Her presence obviously discomfitted him, as if his wife had brought into the room an uncontrollable element.

"Mr. Holmes will do everything he can, Jennie," he said. "Do not fret yourself. Tussy will be back with us soon. She is spreading her own wings for a while, like a young bird, but soon she will return to the nest."

Holmes spoke with deep sincerity: "Let me assure you, Madame, that I will do all within my powers to learn the whereabouts of your daughter, and to restore her to you. Your anxiety is natural; believe me that I have every confidence that your daughter's absence is a passing phenomenon and that you will soon enjoy reunion together."

Karl Marx then spoke abruptly to the house-servant: "Lenchen, help your mistress back to her bed." Mrs. Marx bowed to Holmes, then turned away. Lenchen regarded Marx for a moment as if with defiance. Then she turned and placed her arm around Mrs. Marx's waist, and they both walked slowly through the doorway.

HOLMES AND I WERE WALKING
ALONG HAVERSTOCK HILL.

Marx turned to Holmes apologetically: "Forgive this intrusion, Mr. Holmes, but my wife has been very ill, and Tussy's disappearance has brought on a despair. Our Dr. Donkin is doing all he can, but you see why it is imperative that Tussy come home."

"I quite understand Mrs. Marx's concern, and should now leave, Mr. Marx, and begin my efforts. I am most grateful for all you have told me; it has been helpful."

Karl Marx escorted us to the door below, and soon

Holmes and I were walking along Haverstock Hill. As we hailed a
hansom cab, Holmes directed the driver to the British Museum. "I
shall be consulting books and persons, Watson, and joining
presently the ranks of restless young people of the mind; the
Russians call them, I believe, the 'intelligentsia.' I find it an ugly
word that seems to degrade the intellect." One street before we
reached the great building of books, Holmes left the cab, and I
returned to Baker Street meditating on the old revolutionist, who
seemed to me indeed a pitiful character.

To my surprise, Sherlock Holmes was back in our rooms shortly before dinner. Cheerfully, he accepted a plate of cold mutton
and Hebraic rye bread that Mrs. Hudson kindly offered.

"Watson," he said, "I hope you will accompany me tonight to
a meeting of the Zetetical Society."

"Zetetical? What on the earth is that, Holmes? I hope you're
not planning to immerse yourself in the Oriental cults. You have rid
yourself of cocaine; surely you need no new exotic?"

"Alas, Watson," said Holmes. "In your devotion to medical
studies, you have not done justice to the classics. 'Zetetical' is from
the Greek word for 'seeking,' and tonight we shall be seekers after
truth."

"But what sort of truth, Holmes? I never know what those
chaps are about who talk of seeking Truth in general. And what is
the Zetetical Society?"

"We shall journey, Watson, to the hole and corner that befits
the reformer—in short, to the meeting place of the Zetetical Society
on Great Queen Street, Long Acre, kindly provided by the
Women's Protective and Provident League. There we shall listen to
my newly found friend, Mr. George Bernard Shaw, lecture on 'Is
Socialism the Way Out?' Our fellow Zeteticians, I gather, are all
what they call 'advanced' persons."

"I say, Holmes, I shall find that a bit difficult. I have never
associated with such persons, and indeed regard them as insuffer-
ably arrogant, and usually either rogues, cranks, or unbalanced."

"We shall not have to be unduly 'advanced' ourselves, Watson.
The members are about our age, or a few years younger. To be
sure, they include women as well as men, but all are serious. They
are disciples of Britain's foremost men of science, Mill, Darwin,

Spencer, and Huxley; they admire the men and women of letters, George Eliot, William Morris, and some of them, like Mr. Shaw, want to be writers themselves. Above all, they have a tremendous capacity for indignation, and a desire to recast the world. They are indignant because unhappily married persons find it so difficult to secure divorces; they demand women should be allowed to own property; they also want votes for women, higher wages for workingmen, comfortable houses for all Englishmen, and free schooling through the higher forms. And it seems they are experimenting with socialism."

"I have not gone to a public meeting, Holmes, since I heard Gladstone lambast Disraeli in the election of 1874."

"The Zetetical Society, I assure you, my dear fellow, will be just as exhilarating. I can vouch that you will enjoy Mr. George Bernard Shaw. It will cost us nothing except a few pence for refreshments."

"And who, pray, is Mr. Shaw?" I asked.

"Shaw, my dear Watson, is a young Irishman in his mid-twenties who inhabits the British Museum. He tells me he has been coming there daily for the last five years. During that time he has been writing novels and reading Karl Marx. He says he knows *Das Kapital* in French by heart, and insists it's the only book ever written that explains our modern society."

"How, Holmes, did you meet this Irish disciple of Marx?" I asked, feeling this youthful novelist was still obviously wanting in judgment. "What would make of an Irishman a devil's disciple?"

"Book lovers, my dear Watson, have been comrades in all places and times. I went to the British Museum, searched its catalogue, and asked for Karl Marx's *Capital* and several of his English pamphlets. The librarian told me that young Mr. Shaw, sitting far to the left side in the reading room, unmistakable in his red beard, had asserted a monopoly over Marx's works. In response to the librarian's remonstrances, Mr. Shaw claimed his was not a capitalist monopoly but a socialist one. Therefore, the best the librarian could do was suggest that I approach Mr. Shaw myself, and ask whether I could be allowed to read Karl Marx's book and pamphlets.

"This I did. Shaw rose most courteously. He is a tall man,

indeed as tall as I, with penetrating eyes and a fun-laden face that seems to be masquerading as Mephistopheles. He looks like an actor confident of his audience and speaks with a tone and precision that seems to put his personal imprint on every word. He was delighted to meet another scholar of Marx and suggested we adjourn to the Great Hall where we could talk without disturbing our fellow readers. I did feel, Watson, as if I was trespassing on these faces around me absorbed in Egyptian hieroglyphics and Babylonian cuneiform.

"We introduced ourselves outside. He was pleased to encounter the promising young detective, Sherlock Holmes, and he assured me he was an equally promising writer. I must confess, my dear Watson, that he had some criticism of your two published brochures, but I assure you I told him most emphatically that I disagreed with his criticism. Shaw feels that a detective story is never complete unless it shows how the particular criminal and his crime are a product of the social circumstances under which he was nurtured. I told Shaw that I had learned from Charles Darwin and Alfred Russel Wallace that an individual's character was mainly determined by his ancestral inheritance and that the criminal, in the true sense, was reverting to traits of some primitive forebear. The upshot was that Shaw insisted that I must attend tonight's meeting of the Zetetical Society; he assured me that, even if I didn't learn much, I would enjoy it tremendously. In short, I allowed myself to accept his invitation. Then, as if remembering that the Zetetical Society would do well to have a writer such as yourself present at their meeting, Shaw hastened to add that I must bring my friend Dr. Watson with me, if he is at all willing. 'Who knows?' Shaw added. 'I might appear as a sympathetic character in a memoir in *The Strand* magazine entitled *The Strange Case of the Zetetic Society*. It would please all the Zeteticians who are votaries of the printed word.' "

I remained a bit skeptical. "Holmes," I asked, "is listening to a session of Bohemians, cranks, and crackpots really necessary for finding Miss Eleanor Marx? I recall those marvelous deductions that so quickly led you to identifying the physical traits of a murderer and to solving the murder case."

"I assure you, Watson, I am not indulging in any roundabout

digression. I feel Mr. George Bernard Shaw may help lead us very quickly to a meeting with Eleanor Marx. Since Shaw wished to resume his writing of what he called his fourth unpublished novel, I asked him what journals I might consult to learn the ideas of his fellow Zeteticians. He recommended *Progress,* the *National Reformer,* and *Today.* I promptly secured the latest copies of these journals in the Reading Room. There in the pages of *Progress* was none other than Eleanor Marx herself writing on Russian nihilism, the underground, and the Irish dynamiters. She writes with verve and admiration; she seems to think that, if a man sacrifices himself for an idea, that proves the idea is true. Somewhere in this milieu, Watson, we will find her; and whatever she will be doing, she will be sacrificing herself. But meanwhile, too, she seems to be engaged in controversies of a personal kind. Miss Marx in another short article poked fun at the secularists of the *National Reformer;* she thinks atheism and freethought are of small moment in the 'proletariat's' struggle for emancipation. What is 'proletariat,' Watson? I gather she means the working class, but why insult them with that word which, according to the dictionary, denotes the lazy, nonworking spectators at the Roman circuses? Greater, however, was my surprise when I found that the *National Reformer* has rebutted Miss Marx with a sharp, satirical note written by none other than Mrs. Annie Besant.''

"Mrs. Annie Besant? Who, Holmes, might that be? During my years in India and Afghanistan, I hardly kept informed of actresses and celebrities.''

"Mrs. Annie Besant, my dear Watson, is the most unusual woman in England, the most eloquent orator among her sex, and endowed with great charm and attraction. Five years ago, the newspapers were traducing her in leaders, news stories, and editorials as the misleader of British womanhood. Her husband was Reverend Besant, but Mrs. Besant evolved rebelliously into a militant atheist and an agitator for Malthusian limitations on childbearing. When she finally left his bed and board, taking with her a small daughter, the husband sued for custody of the child, alleging that Mrs. Besant was clearly no fit mother. The judge, Sir George Jessel, no less, who tried the case, was appalled by a defendant who snatched the New Testament from her child lest its coarse passages pollute her mind. The Reverend Besant not unexpectedly won his suit. Mrs. Besant, though recognized to have been a loving mother, lost her child. She is now the heroine of the secularist and women's movements; rumor has it that, abiding by her principles, she has lived in free union with the atheist parliamentarian Charles Bradlaugh. I am apprehensive indeed that Eleanor Marx has evoked the wrath of Mrs. Besant; these two rationalists are most irrational toward one another and clearly some highly emotional division is involved. I could not help feeling they were quarreling over a man. As Darwinians, they should call their struggle with the words—our great man of science used them in his last melancholy book—'sexual selection.' "

HOLMES PRODUCED FROM HIS COAT POCKET A SHEET OF PAPER.

"But what did Mrs. Besant write about Miss Eleanor Marx?"
Holmes slowly produced from his coat pocket a sheet of paper.
"I copied the offensive lines from the *National Reformer.*"

My name is being used by a Miss Eleanor Marx, daughter of Karl
Marx and an inveterate foe of the Freethought Movement, to give
authority to a gross and scandalous libel on Dr. Edward Aveling. She
invented and spread the libel, giving me as its author; she obviously
hopes thereby to introduce discord among the coworkers of the
movement. Dr. Aveling brought the statement to me when it reached
his ears. Irremediable mischief may be caused by such persons as
Miss Eleanor Marx; they are the most useful tools employed by the
Christian foe.

"I say, Holmes," I remarked. "These freethinkers don't seem
to show Christian charity toward each other."
Holmes laughed cheerfully. "A touch, Watson, a touch! No,
Mrs. Besant and Miss Marx certainly don't appear to elevate the
freethinkers' charity."
"And who is this Dr. Aveling, Holmes, over whom the women
seem to be quarreling?"
"I do not know, Watson, but this evening we should learn. Let
us finish our dinner, and then to the Zetetical Society."
The house on Great Queen Street belonging to the Women's
Protective and Provident League was a gloomy, gray three-story
building that seemed to exude a mist of misfortune. I wondered
how many unhappy souls, downcast with their lives, feeling friendless and repudiated by their families, must have come wandering
here to find solace from a stranger's hand. Even Holmes for a
moment seemed to lose his imperturbability and to respond to its
bricked integration of human pain. We entered, and observed a
poster on which was scrawled in red crayon:

Zetetical Society, Speaker: George Bernard Shaw on: "Is Socialism
the Way Out?" Room 118, Tonight, 8:00 P.M.

We proceeded through the dimly lit hallway to the meeting
room, which we surely would have recognized from the sound of
the animated voices that escaped through its open door. About

twenty-five young men and women were milling about, talking, arguing, and laughing with a gaiety I envied. Indeed, I do not think I have ever seen a group of men and women speaking to each other in so natural a way. For a moment I felt envious of them, because, though I was only a few years older than they, the Afghan campaign and my recent bereavement had left me convinced that my youth was far behind me.

Suddenly a tall, red-bearded young man, quite pale, with oversized ears and nose, and a mouth curled but firm, was beside us shaking Holmes's hand heartily, and exclaiming: "I am enormously pleased, my dear Mr. Holmes, that you will be among us seekers tonight. And please do speak up during the discussion period. We then become a dialectical society, for the truth, as Heraclitus and Hegel said, emerges in conflict."

I regarded his loose tweeds, the ragged cuffs, trimmed to respectability, and the thin-worn, exhausted boots. Then turning to me before Holmes could respond, Shaw greeted me exuberantly. "Dr. Watson, my fellow writer, and, I concede, my superior in pure narrative."

I thanked him somewhat guardedly, because I harbored uncertainty as to what unexpected verbal ambush might follow. I asked him what kind of book he was writing.

He answered, "I am a writer of unpublished novels. There are two problems I face: first, my ideas are too far ahead of my time; and, second, I have not yet mastered my craft. But I am working at solving both, and meanwhile my mother kindly maintains me with her singing lessons."

I was really surprised to hear a fully grown, vigorous man acknowledge that he lived through his mother's earnings, and I lamely asked what were the titles of his novels. He declaimed with the precision of an elocution master, giving full value to every syllable, "*Immaturity, Love Among the Artists, The Irrational Knot,* and now I am working on a story of a prizefighter, *Cashel Byron's Profession.*"

I did not know whether to take such titles seriously; was *Immaturity* a record of its author, as *Love Among the Artists* was a next experience in rebellion against middle-class ways? Was *The Irrational Knot* a pamphlet against marriage? I thought to myself,

"My tall, declamatory friend, a term of duty in Afghanistan might bring you to your senses; perhaps you would then write of maturity, rational ties, and sincere love among real people, not the bogus imitation of make-believers." But I only lamely replied that I hoped someday to read one of his novels in print. Abruptly, however, Shaw stalked to the lectern at the front of the room and shook hands with a little man who proved to be the chairman of the meeting.

Mr. Sidney Webb was the chairman's name, as he said in a soft, dull monotone by way of introducing himself. Although his goatee drooped sadly, literally giving him the appearance of a goat, Mr. Webb seemed to exert an authority over the group, which was now attentive. "Our speaker this evening is well known to us all. Mr. George Bernard Shaw is a thorough student of political economy, especially the writings of the German thinker Karl Marx, and much esteemed among us for his encyclopaedic knowledge of music. Tonight, however, he will neither sing nor speak to us of music, but rather discuss the problem that is on the minds of all of us, 'Is Socialism the Answer?' "

Some animated applause greeted the speaker, presumably on the part of those who already knew that socialism was the answer. Then Mr. Shaw began to speak. Within a few minutes, I found myself entranced. His words formed themselves into clearly minted sentences of prose, exact and sharp. Above all, wit pervaded his remarks, which were always reasoned. No metaphors got in the way of the understanding. He began by saying that he would explain why we had a trade cycle that periodically brought misery to great numbers. He explained what he called the labor theory of value, and it seemed common sense to me: That a commodity is worth as much work as you put into it, and that nonproductive classes lived by extracting "surplus value" from the workingmen. He described how the invention of machines in the long run reduced the number of necessary workers, and how with unemployment capitalists found it ever harder to realize their "surplus value." I recalled how my grandfather, an old Chartist, once told me when I was a child how the new machines had one day deprived him of his job in the Edinburgh mill.

But then Mr. Shaw proceeded to describe how socialism would

solve everything. Having had some experience with both military and civilian bureaucracies, I could not leap into an enthusiastic welcome of Mr. Shaw's proposed answer. What my old professor called a *non sequitur* seemed to be at the heart of his argument. Nevertheless, his eloquence carried me along as he described the renaissance that socialism would bring to "Merrie England"; the arts and sciences would flourish. "Your unpublished books would be published," I thought to myself, perhaps cynically. Men and women generally would wed whomsoever they chose, unimpeded by the artificial barriers of class. The young audience, I observed, seemed to respond to the last forecast with flushed cheeks and sparkling eyes. I glanced at Sherlock Holmes; his eyes continually surveyed the listeners and occasionally stopped to examine someone closely. The speaker ended; we joined willingly and cheerfully in the applause. Then the chairman called for questions.

First, a scholarly looking middle-aged man rose and asked Mr. Shaw why a painting might be worth so much money when it was the product of only a few hours' work.

Shaw was quiet for a few moments, then said dramatically and with the most disarming charm: "My dear Reverend Wicksteed, I really don't know the answer to that and must think about it some more. It was the industrial workingmen and their products in factories I was thinking about. I don't know how the labor theory of value applies to works of art. But I can assure you, as an artist myself trying to persuade capitalist publishing houses to publish my own novels, the most penetrating studies of English middle-class society since Henry Fielding, I should be pleased that if, instead of placing their value at zero, they would pay me a value corresponding to the labor-time of my novel-writing."

Political Economy Among the Artists, I ruminated, has its problems.

Then another questioner arose, short, broad-shouldered, with heavy features and carefully combed hair. There was a certain theatricality in his appearance and utterance. He gave the impression that, if possible, his question would impale the lecturer.

"I am not concerned, Mr. Speaker," he began, "with the dialectical niceties of the labor theory of value. They make no difference as far as the desirability or undesirability of socialism is

40

concerned. What I wish to know is whether the people will thrive and work, or grow lazy and degenerate, under socialism. The Roman proletariat degenerated into a lazy and lascivious mob when their food, shelter, baths, and circuses were provided. You and I, Mr. Shaw, are both Darwinists, and surely you will recall Darwin's discussion of how societies, like species, degenerate. Would socialism, with its guarantees of livelihood to all, reverse all that was healthy in natural selection?''

Who was this man, I wondered, who argued so well for the place of evil in this world, and who seemed himself to exude an intimation of evil? I learned his name at once, for Shaw responded: "Dr. Edward Aveling is an unquestioned authority in zoological science. I have read his articles on Darwin with much pleasure and admire the energy he has brought to the diffusion of scientific knowledge. But Rome fell not because of the Roman proletariat but because there was no Roman proletariat. Rome failed to advance into the next historical stage, that of capitalism; and in history, if you don't advance, you go backwards. Rome failed to advance toward science and invention; it had no Newtons, no Galileos, no Descartes, no Leibnizes. And Christianity didn't help matters when it turned men's minds to defining the undefinable Trinity. We can trust to the union of science and socialism to counteract the miasma of decadence that has come on capitalistic Europe.''

A burst of applause issued from the now enthusiastic audience. The chairman jumped to his feet, expressed the thanks of the Society to Mr. Shaw, and announced tea and refreshments.

Holmes moved quickly toward Aveling, taking me with him. "Dr. Aveling," he said, "I was much interested in the view you presented. Could you direct me to some further reading?''

Edward Aveling regarded Holmes acutely. Just then, George Bernard Shaw joined us saying with gusto, "Have you been introduced? Dr. Aveling, this is my friend Sherlock Holmes, and his collaborator, Dr. John Watson. You might say that Mr. Holmes represents the Darwinian scientific method in the study of crime; he has collected cases and criminals in a Baconian spirit, and his reconstructions from a few shreds of evidence will rival those of the paleontologist. His associate, Dr. Watson, is what Huxley has been to Darwin—the chronicler, defender, and expositor of Sherlock Holmes.''

Dr. Aveling, holding a small book in one hand, extended the other to Holmes, and shook Holmes's hand vigorously, and repeated the gesture with me. "I should almost think you were an American," remarked Holmes, "but your accent is specifically London clerical." Aveling laughed and said: "I was waiting for you to apply your deductive science to me. What else would you infer?''

"I would also infer that you have recently been in communication with Charles Darwin, but not altogether successfully in your aim, and that some young woman, most inexperienced in the household arts, has tried to mend your garments.''

I looked at Holmes with amazement. Aveling and Shaw both stood speechless. "I say, old man," said Shaw, "you must have been listening to some of the gossips who come to our meetings. Don't pay attention to them. Think of what they say about me. Probably they think I am a preacher and practitioner of free love because I affirm that the *Communist Manifesto* of Marx and Engels is the greatest political pamphlet ever written, and that I intend to model my political language on theirs, and not on either Burke, Fox, Disraeli, or Gladstone. Actually, my dear Holmes, I am still *virgo intacta.*''

Dr. Aveling looked at Holmes with a cold scrutiny, as if he were examining him on a microscopic slide. "Might you explain, if you please, Mr. Holmes, the syllogisms in your deductions?''

"Elementary you will find them, Dr. Aveling. I observe that you have in your hand a copy of a new book by yourself, *The Student's Darwin*. But apart from your name the cover adds nothing more, no title of an introduction by Charles Darwin himself. But surely a young author such as yourself would have sought the approval or authorization of Darwin personally. Your publishers, the Freethought Association, have doubtlessly urged you to invite the name of the great scientist directly. I conclude that you thus wrote to Darwin, but that he declined. Meanwhile, my attention was drawn to the amateurish but laborious effort to sew buttons on your suit. They are ill-fitting and poorly sewn; moreover, where a man would have first sewn the center, most used buttonholes, the peripheral ones were mended instead and the supply of replacements was exhausted. That suggests a young person inexperienced in the proper maintenance of a man's clothes."

Edward Aveling regarded Holmes questioningly, "I am sure we will meet again, Mr. Holmes," he said, "and Dr. Watson too." He bowed and left.

Shaw cheerfully tried to undo the slight strain in the atmosphere.

He resumed chatting with Holmes and me about the labor theory of value, and whether it applied to the labor-power and labor-time of a consulting detective. At this juncture, a tall, thin, strangely wraithlike but beautiful young woman approached us; she bore herself with as much dignity and grace as I had ever seen combined. She said not a word, but regarded Shaw questioningly with her clear dark eyes. Even Shaw, always alert to the comic aspect of things, responded as if to a regal command.

"Miss Beatrice Potter, may I present to you Mr. Sherlock Holmes and his friend and chronicler, Dr. John Watson?"

We bowed to Miss Beatrice Potter, who regarded us at once courteously and critically.

"How fortunate you have come, Mr. Holmes and Dr. Watson, to this evening's meeting, for Shaw, Webb, and I are discussing whether to found a socialist club of a very new kind. It would be most helpful to know your views."

"Pray, Miss Potter," said Holmes, "am I to understand that you, like Shaw, have accepted Karl Marx's labor theory of value and now wish to found a Marxist society?"

Beatrice Potter laughed and waved her hand as if dismissing some academic disputation.

"Mr. Holmes," she said, "I think our English economist, Jevons, has clarified that whole subject of value so thoroughly as to make Marx's theory as obsolete as a medieval metaphysical gossamer. As for Shaw, with every additional lecture he gives on the subject, he sees more fallacies in Marx."

"Some people learn by doing; I learn by lecturing," said Shaw.

"But what if the listener only heard last month's lecture, and not your latest? His political decision would have been influenced by ideas that the baker himself had irresponsibly advertised as fully baked," said Holmes.

"My dear Holmes, thinking is beset with the same risks as every activity in the struggle for existence. It is backed by no guarantee, yet the human species is doing better than its unthinking rivals."

Miss Potter remarked, "You should hear Eleanor Marx on the subject. She maintains the Marxist socialist program is a deduction from the basic laws of social science and that those who disagree with Marx, as I do, are simply not social scientists. She thinks every socialist must repudiate religion categorically. I think our new socialist club should limit its concern for reform to economic and political questions. We should not undertake to prescribe a program for morals or philosophy; we shall have nothing to do with atheist, agnostic, or anti-Christian propaganda."

"Eleanor Marx is more anti-Christian than her father ever was," Shaw observed.

"That's true. She has little respect for Jesus, who, she says, was a weak-headed dreamer who had not the slightest understanding of the economic and political problems of the Roman Empire. She forgets that the British working class is Christian and religious; half the trade-union leaders learned to speak as Methodist lay preachers. How can a Marxist party, wrapped in German atheism, hope to convert the British worker?"

Holmes remarked, "The British worker might well admire Eleanor Marx, like her father, for her sincerity. The British worker admired John Stuart Mill, who was scarcely a Christian in philosophy."

"The philosophic radicals, however, Mr. Holmes," replied Miss Potter, "did not make irreligion a part of their political program. And they lived perfectly conventional personal lives. Even Mill did not challenge bourgeois morality when he fell in love with Mrs. Helen Taylor. He abided by the customary code, and thereby showed the politician's respect for the sensibilities of the people. In short, Mr. Holmes, we propose to be empirical British politicians, not Hegelian Talmudists."

"Have you met either Mr. Marx or Mr. Engels?" asked Holmes.

"Neither," said Miss Potter. "Nor do I wish to. They say the workers will emancipate themselves. We say that's patent nonsense.

The workers need ideas; we'll provide them with all they need and more. We'll work with all and sundry, with liberals, conservatives, manufacturers, colliers, and workingmen. If the conservative ruler of Birmingham, Joseph Chamberlain, would wish to, we'd accept him as our leader. Eleanor Marx regards that as a socialist sin; she wants socialists to keep their class purity and says that Ferdinand Lassalle let himself be hoodwinked by Bismarck. That's Marxist silliness. What's important is to spread socialist solutions, not to provoke reaction by incantations about 'dictatorship of the proletariat.' Lassalle helped get the universal franchise for the German workers—more than Marx ever did keeping his revolutionary purity unsullied."

"Have you seen Eleanor Marx recently?" Shaw queried.

"I met her yesterday in the refreshment room at the British Museum," Beatrice Potter replied. "She looked as if she has missed out on her sleep and keeps working through admixtures of coffee, tea, and tobacco. She could be lovely if she chose, but with her uncombed hair and unwashed appearance, I would never want her to address a public meeting held under my society's auspices."

"And what will you call your society?" asked Holmes.

Beatrice Potter pondered thoughtfully. "I don't quite know."

Shaw interrupted, "I shall be godfather to your society. I have just the right name. There was a Roman general I read about at school. His name was Fabius; they called him 'Cunctator the delayer,' because he wore old Hannibal down by never risking his Roman troops in direct battle with the better Carthaginian army. Gradually he decimated and destroyed the enemy. Thus we would do to the stronger, richer, and better equipped capitalist forces. We shall be Fabian socialists who will gradually diminish and defeat the bourgeois defenders. Our socialists will not die on barricades; they will triumph instead as cabinet ministers in parliaments. Fabians then we are."

Beatrice Potter said, smilingly, "Shaw, I feel you have been my Socratic midwife tonight." She left us to converse with others.

Shaw turned to Holmes. "I say, Holmes, would you and Watson celebrate the conception of this new Fabian society by coming along to the Wheatsheaf Vegetarian Restaurant in Rathbury Place? I take my dinners there; they usually cost me only a few pence. If you have already had yours, you could have a vegetable pudding or milk with scones."

Holmes and I were both obviously pleased by the invitation, and we walked with the speaker to his vegetarian haunt. We found a small restaurant, extremely neat, with workmanlike tables and chairs, all simple and unadorned. On the wall hung a curious selection of prints—the agitator for women's rights, Mary Wollstonecraft, the poet Shelley, and the Greek philosopher Pythagoras.

"You may be surprised, Dr. Watson," said Shaw, "at the inclusion of Pythagoras. But, besides his famous geometrical proof that I could never understand, he was the first vegetarian socialist."

I thanked him for this unusual item of erudition.

Soon Holmes and I were enjoying our vegetable puddings, and Shaw was consuming with much appetite something called a "mushroom cutlet." Shaw's flow of discourse never halted. He talked of his novels, and his hope of creating a new novel of contemporary ideas; he had not, he said, the genius of a Dickens to make real and interesting the tragedies and characters of the lowliest souls, but what he could do was to depict the ferment of the "New Thought" among the intelligent members of the middle class. "There is a drama in the rise and triumph of new ideas that no British writer has yet captured—not the tawdry, fraudulent tinsel that Disraeli displayed, or even the romanticized aspiration of George Eliot, but the ideas themselves, in all their pure clarity, calling forth a more rational conception of human intercourse."

His sentences were enunciated with such grammatical perfection and periodic structure that I ventured to suggest that he might try writing plays. "I have thought of that myself, old chap, especially as the pile of my rejected novels grows toward the ceiling. In fact, a few of us have organized a drama reading circle in which we do the parts ourselves; next week, we are reading a wonderful play by the greatest living playwright of Europe, the Norwegian Henrik Ibsen."

Holmes remarked dryly that he had not heard of him.

"Then you will shortly, my dear fellow, as William Archer and Eleanor Marx are both working on translations. Ibsen is the man who sweeps away the romantic poppycock that has bestrewn the stage. He is the new Prometheus. He dares to challenge the myths of the family and the social system; and he does so with a command of the dramatic technique that makes all our London playwrights seem like stagehand novices.''

"And what manner of work," said Holmes, "does Eleanor Marx do? Does she bear worthily the mantle of the Karl Marx of whom you have spoken so persuasively?''

Shaw glanced at us with a confiding expression. "Eleanor is Karl Marx's daughter, and she has all his dash, courage, tenacity, and union of clear seeing and thinking in the present together with a vision of the future. But she also has her mother's instinct for self-immolation; I hear that her mother went through agonies of physical suffering during their early years of marriage. Karl Marx was even less able to live comfortably by his pen than I am. I used to meet Eleanor quite often at the British Museum, and we'd talk politics and plays. One evening she took me to the house of Friedrich Engels, the collaborator of Marx; you really ought to go to one of Engels's 'at homes,' and hear the old warrior arguing about philosophy with Belfort Bax, telling off Hyndman as an unprincipled plagiarist, and for a climax singing 'The Vicar of Bray.' Up to that evening, I had been cultivating romantic dreams about love with the dreamy-eyed Eleanor who would be the 'blessed damozel' of my penurious existence. But at Engels's house we met Dr. Edward Aveling, and my dream turned to nothingness.''

"Do you mean," I said, "that the Dr. Aveling whom we met is the fiancé of Miss Eleanor Marx?'' There was a tone of disbelief in my question, for Aveling had made such an unpleasant impression on me. Shaw looked at me and Holmes quizzically.

"Dr. Edward B. Aveling is a man of brilliance with genuine attainments in zoology. He is a doctor of science of University College at the University of London. But he is a man who practices a free ethic as far as money and women are concerned. He will borrow from every acquaintance on those frequent occasions when he chances to be without funds; he has been known to repay loans but only under duress. He practices a kind of 'individualistic expropriation,' as he calls it. He is said to be separated from his wife; some say she expelled him for his atheist views, while others have it that he left her after having expropriated her alienable fortune. He says that, unprepossessing though he looks, he could win any woman he desires, even were a rival Don Juan to have the advantages of a handsome appearance. A half-hour is all he needs. He has what you might call a zoological approach to life. Some women find him sinister and repulsive and have refused to be present at Engels's 'at homes' when they knew that Aveling would be there. Others are drawn ineluctably toward him. I fear that Eleanor Marx is one of those. That in him which others find evil is for her the occasion of a redemption by the good. She loves the sound of his voice as he reads Shelley's poems and thinks that anyone with such love for beauty must have a beautiful soul.''

Holmes and I both sat silently. Then Holmes said: ''I hope Miss Eleanor Marx will not come to grief.''

Shaw did not respond. Then, quickly regaining all his zest, he said: ''You can meet her at a reading we shall be giving this Saturday afternoon of *A Doll's House*. Eleanor, Aveling, and I are all reading parts. It will be at the home of my good friend William Morris, and you will be my guests again. Three o'clock, at Hammersmith; here, copy the address down.''

Holmes and I returned to Baker Street by hansom cab. More taciturn than usual, Holmes sat by the fire brooding. I felt I should cheer him, and said in a congratulatory voice: ''Well, Holmes, this case seems to be solving itself quickly, thanks to your expeditions; whatever mystery there was seems to have dissolved. Eleanor Marx is probably residing with Dr. Edward Aveling. When you have verified that fact, and thus informed Mr. Frederick Engels, your work will be done. You have moved through this Bohemian political underworld with a remarkable instinct.''

Holmes replied gloomily: ''Would it were so, Watson. But finding Eleanor Marx is the easiest portion of our task. It is getting her to leave the home and person of Dr. Edward Aveling that will probably be extraordinarily difficult. For the poor girl has in all likelihood embroiled her feelings irrevocably with Aveling. Where others see a man whose abilities are at the behest of evil, she sees one, whom she loves all the more, to transmute. You and I learned something of what can inspire a Jewish woman, and how she, in turn, can inspire, in the case of 'the Woman' and your king of Bohemia."

"Irene Adler?" I said, lapsing into indiscretion by mentioning her name.

Homes said nothing.

"Shaw," he then replied, "obviously expects that we shall have a difficult case on our hands and that we must not wait too long."

"But Holmes!" I cried. "Shaw knows nothing of your search for Eleanor Marx. To him we are two inquirers, curious concerning the latest fashions among young Bohemian thinkers."

"My dear Watson," said Holmes. "Perhaps he thought that for a few minutes. Obviously, however, he has known for some time that Edward Aveling has Eleanor Marx in his physical possession. As a man of honor, he can say nothing explicitly. Clearly, however, he has been waiting for Karl Marx to take some step to find his daughter, and has been expecting that Engels, the 'General,' would contrive some strategic plan. And when Mr. Sherlock Holmes, the consulting detective, suddenly appears in the library of the British Museum, animated by a newborn desire to master the theories of Karl Marx, George Bernard Shaw is obviously delighted that Marx and Engels are doing something to retrieve Eleanor before she blunders hopelessly, and he is pleased to help Mr. Sherlock Holmes most directly to bring his search to a possible consummation. All this Shaw does honorably as part of his proselytizing for the new culture and philosophy; no unlikelier proselytes have probably ever come his way, he well realizes, than you or I. For all his cordiality to Aveling, Shaw recognizes the sinister component in Aveling's character; they may profess the same daring impulses in philosophy, they may render homage together to Darwin as the guide to the new science and to Shelley as the prophet of the new morality; both may make a fetish of the word 'new,' and Shaw may acknowledge Aveling as a new comrade in the socialism toward which he feels himself drawn. But Shaw inwardly cannot acquiesce to seeing Eleanor Marx reduced to the status of an emotionally servile and victimized person. Well, Watson, we have much to digest of this evening's provender of new socialism and new morality. I shall indulge myself in a last pipe of this new Virginian tobacco, adorned by the countenance of Thomas Jefferson, and after imbibing the smoke of its human equality, I shall then retire for the night."

Holmes was again already gone when I arose much refreshed by sleep after the evening's intellectual adventure. I wondered what Holmes might be about and then went off to St. Bartholomew's Hospital to serve as consulting physician for the afternoon in their tropical diseases section. My Indian experience had qualified me in the hospital's eyes to minister to Malays run amuck, lepers from the South Pacific, Hindus sick after eating meat, and Moslems befuddled by whiskey. When I had returned to Baker Street, and Mrs. Hudson was kindly serving a dinner of New Zealand lamb, the door opened and Holmes, looking somewhat worn, dropped into his chair.

"It has been a highly academic day for me, Watson," he said, "but not unrewarding."

"Why, Holmes, have you been to the British Museum Library again?"

"No, Watson, I resisted the temptation to turn bookworm, and to spend twenty years, as Karl Marx did, in daily visitations to the library. But I have been studying the ways of university coaches and their fledglings. I journeyed today to the building of the University College of the University of London. I paused for a few minutes to penetrate its basement to inspect the taxidermized body of the late Jeremy Bentham, the eccentric philosopher who instructed us all that the good is 'the greatest hap-

LOOKING WORN, HE DROPPED INTO HIS CHAIR.

piness of the greatest number.' He wrote many books, none of which I have read, I confess, my dear Watson, but one of which, on criminal law, I perused. I then called upon the bursar, and told him that I was thinking of taking a degree in mathematics or zoology, but that in my rustiness, due to my absence for several years from academic studies, I would require a coach.

" 'We have several fine coaches,' he replied, 'who have been extraordinarily successful in preparing pupils both for matriculation and degree examinations. Two of them are noted young scientists as well. They are Robert Owen Moriarty in mathematics and Edward B. Aveling in zoology. They use the east classroom on the third floor, and I advise you to proceed there directly. They won't arrive till the afternoon, but their pupils use the rooms for their studies.'

"I went to the east room, where I found several students poring over their books, and some of them filling foolscap with arrays of strange symbols. One of them got up, stretched his arms, and said: 'That Moriarty thinks we are utter fools if we can't expound Sylvester's proof of Newton's Rule, but I wish he'd teach us something of Weierstrass and Cauchy's ideas. Maybe Karl Pearson will change things here if he gets the professorship he's after. Anyone join me at the Common Room for some tea?' Several men arose, and as they went along, invited me to assist in their enclave.

"The Common Room was a comfortable small chamber midway on the floor where a small elderly maid dispensed tea and scones. I told my hosts my name was Holmes and that I was thinking of working under either Moriarty or Aveling. One of them, a short dark-haired man with the pale face of a scholarly Jew and looking as if he stepped out of one of Rembrandt's paintings of the Ghetto, said: 'You couldn't pick two more brilliant, or more corrupt men.' I was surprised by such forthrightness. The man, whose name was Brodetsky, said: 'Moriarty makes the solution of every equation the fulcrum for a reflection on human stupidity. There has never been a mathematician in Parliament, he notes, nor a minister who could reason logically. It awaits for the men of intellect, he declares, to join in a conspiracy to rule as once the Pythagorean order, the first collectivity of mathematicians, aspired. And to achieve that aim, says Moriarty, every means would be justified, just as in mathematics when you can't solve an equation by direct logical deduction you rely on techniques of approximation. Moriarty believes too that just as university students in Russia turned into terrorist assassins and murdered the Czar, so likewise British university students will organize first as a criminal gang to demoralize society and thus prepare the advent of a scientific order. That's the political philosophy of Professor Robert Owen Moriarty.'*

" 'Robert Owen Moriarty!'' I couldn't help but exclaim.

" 'Yes, Holmes,' said Brodetsky. 'Moriarty's father was an enthusiast for Robert Owen and his scheme for covering the earth with communistic parallelogram colonies. A lot of mathematicians would like to find a generalized social equation with a simple solution for all problems, and anyone who can't think likewise they regard as a surd intruder.'

" 'And what of Aveling?' I asked with the tone of a student inquirer.

" 'Thomson here is doing his microscopic preparations under Aveling, and he can tell you about him,' said Brodetsky, indicating a tall, Calvinist-featured, blond-haired man to his left.

"The designated Thomson, however, was strangely reluctant to assess his coach.

" 'I do not know Aveling,' he said. 'None of us really does. He does the demonstrations well, but seems to have lost any desire to continue research of his own. While we do our drawings, he will sit quietly reading a copy of the *National Reformer, Justice,* or Shelley's *Poems.* He does not stay for discussions, but leaves the

---

*Subsequent scholarly literature has evinced a continuing sympathy among "intellectuals" for Professor Moriarty. Moreover, a certain confusion has arisen concerning the Christian names of Professor Robert Owen Moriarty. For this my own account of the reappearance of Mr. Sherlock Holmes several years after his presumed death is chiefly responsible. Under the strains I felt at that time, and the severities of my public controversy with Colonel James Moriarty, the professor's brother, I mistakenly recorded Holmes as having referred to the professor as "Professor James Moriarty." My blunder was an example of how our feelings can distort our memory, as Professor Alexander Bain used to explain to us in his lectures on psychology. Mindful also as I was of the esteem in which the reformer Robert Owen is held by trade unionists, socialists, and spiritualists, I was disinclined to associate his illustrious name with that of the criminal Professor Moriarty, and allowed myself instead to omit it from my recollection.

college directly; he has been seen walking in the worst parts of Whitechapel and Spitalfields, down Flower and Dean Streets and Dorset Street—the most evil thoroughfare in the city. During the last weeks, however, he has been very chummy with Moriarty. As I was waiting near the door before the coaching session began, I heard Moriarty saying to him teasingly: "You're the first Marxist to be converted by the daughter rather than the father, and to become a socialist for purely capitalistic reasons." It fixed itself in my mind because of the strange paradoxes. Then Aveling replied: "And you, Moriarty, are the only integral Bakuninist of Britain. The old Russian said the bandit chief was the model revolutionist; you would centralize the bands into one secret order obedient to you, their Jesuit commanding general." If I hadn't heard Prince Kropotkin, a fine geologist, lecturing a few weeks ago on the geography and animal life of Siberia, and then afterwards in the Common Room explaining the difference between his anarchism and Bakunin's, I shouldn't have understood what Aveling was talking about. As it was, I felt uneasy at what I heard. Huxley has been talking much lately of the nightmare that the scientific standpoint has brought into the lives of many idealistic persons. Aveling and Moriarty both seem to be rejoicing in the nightmare.

" 'Last week Aveling brought a young woman to attend the lecture he was giving on the zoological evidence for Charles Darwin's hypothesis of natural selection. She seemed a very spiritual sort of person, and raised questions afterward concerning the power of man's reason to bring an end to the prehistory of cruel, unconscious, natural selection, and to substitute for it instead man's conscious guidance of his evolution. I would not have taken much notice of her, except that at the end of the classroom hour I heard Aveling introduce her to Moriarty as Mrs. Aveling. So perhaps there will be a happier evolution for Dr. Aveling, though Lankester has been telling the British Association that extinction and retrogression are far more the frequent phenomena in zoology and sociology alike.'

"Do you know, Watson, I haven't listened to so fascinating a philosophic discussion in years. These students at University College live in an intellectual world more searching and inquiring than that I knew at my college. Cambridge, like Oxford, buzzed about the tractarians, Keble and Newman. I found those theologians unreadable, pompous, and devoid of that respect for observations, hypotheses, predictions, and verifications that become second nature to the student of the sciences. I was regarded, Watson, as an eccentric because such studies as chemistry and geology attracted me. The master of our college still rated very low anyone who showed no ambition to read Plato in the original Greek. But these University College men, with their Darwin and Huxley, are the predestined inheritors of a world whose intellectual achievements will make the metaphysics of Plato and Aristotle as obsolete as their gods and goddesses."

"I wish I could agree with you wholeheartedly, Holmes," I replied, "on all the happy consequences of the scientific world-view. But without a basis in religious belief, the moral sense, in my view, becomes maimed and atrophies. As you have described them, both Robert Owen Moriarty and Edward Aveling are men of science, well enough esteemed for their abilities, though neither of them seems to be a person of a correspondingly high character. Both of them, I gather, are devoid of religion. I fear that, if science displaces religion, there will be a widespread moral decline in society; Britain will renounce its imperial mission and recede into the condition of mediocrity and a commitment to the second-rate. Without the guidance of a religious moral sense, science itself becomes the device of evil; knowledge without the ethical spirit can be more destructive than the ethical spirit without science; the first is an inner corruption, the second is innocence."

Holmes was silent for a moment. "I shall not argue with you, my dear Watson, about the transcendental. I was, as you may remember, an utter failure as a clergyman in my pathetic effort to deceive Miss Irene Adler."

The following morning Holmes once again had disappeared before I was ready for breakfast. I worried lest he had forgotten that this was the day we were to attend the reading of a play by a Norwegian writer at the home of our sturdy poet of medieval chivalry, William Morris. I have enjoyed the latter's sagas of the Norse warriors, men of courage and simple ideas, and I found it difficult to comprehend what this modern bard could feel in common with the likes of George Bernard Shaw and Edward Aveling,

Bohemian anarchists with little sense of manly battle, and with no appreciation of the lance and sword that prove one's mettle. Valor is the virtue I most admire, and the talkative Shaw and the parasitic Aveling seemed to have precious little of it.

"CIVILIZATION, I APPREHEND, IS A MATTER OF RECORDS AND FILES."

Shortly before two o'clock, however, Holmes returned.

"Watson," he began cheerily, "civilization, I apprehend, is a matter of records and files. Primitive men moved about encumbered by no document, no residue from the past engrafted on paper, parchment, or even stone. Civilized men, however, leave their signs in the halls of registry, where a few entries chronicle their birth, marriage, and death. And there, having spent several hours of research, I have emerged with a brief biography of Edward Bibbins Aveling: Born on the 29th of November 1849 at 6 Nelson Terrace in the borough of Hackney—the fifth child of Reverend Thomas W. B. Aveling and his wife Mary Ann. The father was the minister at the Independent Chapel in Robinson's Row, High Street. The son Edward was married on the 30th of July 1872 at the Union Chapel, Islington, to a Miss Isabel Campbell Frank, the child of a deceased poulterer.

"I took a cab to the poultry establishment, which still exists, and inquired where I might find the children of the old owner, indicating the possibility that I was a long-lost, welcome relative. 'Belle,' they told me, had been living alone on Brooke Street, in Holborn, ever since her husband left her, after having spent all her money. 'Poor Belle,' they said. 'Her father would have seen through that adventurer who courted her, but the poor girl was innocent of the ways of the world, and the reverend's son plucked her like we would a chicken.' Then to Brooke Street where indeed I found Mrs. Isabel Aveling, a sad, round-faced gentlewoman, sitting surrounded by her family photographs, evidently living on her share of the annual income of her father's properties in trust. Still bewildered by all that had happened—the collapse of her personal life—she sees virtually no one and was glad to talk to me when I told her I was a scholar inquiring into the marriage institution among Christian folk, with the hope of writing a monograph on the marriages of ministers' sons. She told me Aveling ran through her dowry within a few months, and then threatened to leave her altogether if she did not transfer her annuity to him. Meanwhile, she had learned things of her husband's character that she could never bring herself to utter, nor could she even hint at their nature to the world—deeds so shocking that mere knowledge of them stained a person's soul. Aveling finally left her; she has heard he now write atheistic propaganda. When she met him, he was a brilliant, promising physiologist, who attended his father's sermons. Then Edward repudiated the Reverend Aveling and affirmed that, as for himself, the chief aim of science would be to liberate man from religion and to emancipate the body forever from the trammels of religious morality.

"I felt a sympathy, Watson, for the simple, lonely woman. Her life appeared shattered. How she must have rejoiced at the wonderful young man she was marrying, this extraordinary spirit, Dr. Edward Aveling, who was consecrating his life to science, to the knowledge and the glory of God's works. And then to find that she had embraced a man of sin, not a repentant, nor a weakling, but one who found his pride and fulfillment in sin.

"But the hour for Ibsen is approaching, my dear Watson. Let us begin our journey to Hammersmith."

Chapter Three

elmscott House has become a virtual shrine for socialists. Every religion naturally has its holy places. The Moslem, however poverty-subdued he may be, tries at least once in his lifetime to journey to Mecca and behold the sacred Kaaba; every Roman Catholic feels a mystical joy as he sees with his own eyes the Mother Church at Rome, even as every Jew feels himself a Hebrew again when he walks in the sacred precincts of Jerusalem. Thus, ardent young socialists have gazed at the three-story house in Hammersmith from which emanated the communistic dream of Friar John Ball in the fourteenth century that was transmitted to William Morris in the nineteenth and awaited realization in the twentieth.

I, on the other hand, perceived prosaically a plain three-story building, with two gabled attics, looking out through a fine row of elm trees on the Thames River. Several young people were already inside and talking earnestly with each other. Shown up the staircase to the first floor, we walked on a lovely carpet, surrounded by a world of wallpapers decorated with the most exquisitely formed and colored flowers. I felt the sense of sacrilege that every child feels when it first enters a museum: beauty must be experienced to be enjoyed, yet every approach diminishes its physical existence. The ethereal attribute of the house was enhanced by pictures placed at inobtrusive intervals that were all painted in the style called Pre-Raphaelite, and most depicted a woman. She had an angel-like, olive-complexioned face that was enveloped in long, flowing black hair; a gown delicately endraped her body, as if the fabrics felt privileged in their embrace. Her whole person suggested that her transcendent spirit was impatient with its earthly limitation. Suddenly, the apparition approached us in the form of our hostess: "I am Mrs. Morris." Even Holmes was taken aback by her sheer beauty. "You know almost everybody, I'm sure," she said. Then Mr. William Morris greeted us. A stocky, broad-shouldered man, he gave the impression of immense physical vigor and strength. A childlike face with deep hazel eyes looked from behind an unkempt, somewhat straggly beard. His hair was only partially combed. Morris wore a blue suit, matched by a blue, cloudlike shirt that announced to all and sundry: "I am a handicraftsman."

Morris greeted Holmes and myself warmly, and reiterated that we had done the socialist movement a service by dispelling the crude suggestion in the Jefferson Hope case that socialist societies had been involved in cruel murder. Holmes remarked to Morris that evidently Karl Marx's *Capital* was having a deep influence in guiding young people to socialism.

"Not as far as I am concerned!" boomed Morris. "I find Marx's theories either boring or false. I subscribe to no Hegelian dialectic; I don't even know what it means. Marx's materialistic conception of history is patently false; none of us middle-class people would be here tonight if it were true. I am a prosperous manufacturer, and proud to be so. You must drop by at our showrooms, Mr. Holmes, at 449 Oxford Street, and study the samples we keep there of our fabrics, furniture, and pottery. I have decorated churches, factories, and St. James's Palace. I believe in the beauty of work, Mr. Holmes, and in the use of one's hands to create. Marx, on the other hand, advocates toil and worships the machine. The Middle Ages, in my opinion, was a time when the artisan loved his work, and his work was his art; I think the workmen in the medieval towns were happier than they have ever been in modern times. To me the Industrial Revolution was an industrial counterrevolution as far as the nature of man is concerned.

"But Marx despises the Middle Ages; he prostrates himself before his bogus 'historical necessity,' and he calls me a Utopian socialist. To me socialism is a consummation of man's artistic impulse; to Marx, it's a mechanical by-product of machinery. No,

Mr. Holmes, I am no Marxist; and, let me whisper to you, I don't think his daughter Eleanor is either. There she is in the corner talking with Irene Adler."

Holmes's face suddenly grew white and taut. He drew me with him, and we stood face to face with those two remarkable women, Eleanor Marx and Irene Adler.

Miss Adler's face sparkled. "Dear Mr. Holmes, at last we meet, and you are not bedecked in your silly costume as a minister. Of course, I could have exposed you by reciting to you lines from the Old Testament; your hopeless ignorance of Genesis and Exodus would have betrayed you. But I enjoyed your costumery immensely. How surprised I am, however, to see you at a socialist reading. And Dr. Watson, may I welcome you, a biographer greater than Boswell, and present you to Miss Eleanor Marx?"

This then was she, Tussy, the beloved of her father, the child filled with idealism and love for humanity, and yet herself enchained to an evil-powered man. Her eyes were luminous, dark orbs that looked at one appealingly; her hair, in long black waves, came to her shoulders. She was well proportioned without conveying the massive, physical determination of her father. There was a slight swarthiness to her face; I recalled they called her father "the Moor." A premonition filled me of a child raised on fairy tales who would find herself inexorably impelled to disaster because in the real world she would follow the roads of her world of make-believe.

Eleanor Marx greeted Holmes and myself. "Dr. Watson," she said, "I am a writer, too. But in your accounts of Mr. Holmes's work, entrancing though they are, I find you have been entirely unaffected by the whole new movement of literature, of Ibsen, Flaubert, Strindberg. Your *Study in Scarlet* is a classic, in spite of your ignorance of social movements. You wrote with a just indignation against the Mormons' humiliation of the young heroine. But that is not enough. One must study the movement's social sources. Why did so many New England women accept a polygamous status? Not because some religious zealot overcame their reason. No, they were lonely, because the unmarried men, the bachelors, were deserting them, going West to the mining and land frontiers, speculating for quick capitalistic accumulations. Were they then to reconcile themselves to lives totally devoid of love and mother-hood? Their revolt to be sure, took an irrational form; it was a backward step. I would rather they had lived in free unions in New England, but, in that case, their society would have banished them.''

I mumbled something to the effect that I was writing of human beings, of persons and their deeds, emotions, and thoughts and that I was not arguing for any theory of society.

Eleanor Marx waved her hand almost imperiously. When it was a question of social philosophy, she obviously felt superior to all criticism; the father lived in the daughter. "Dr. Watson," she said, "you are, despite yourself, one of us. Every true artist finds his place in our ranks. In one gesture at the end of *The Sign of Four,* you proclaimed your rejection of the values of the bourgeois system.''

I stood astounded, I fear, perhaps vacant-faced, or open-mouthed. Who could attribute such leveling notions to myself, a surgeon of the Indian Army, who had gone loyally and voluntarily through exhausting campaigns to safeguard and extend Her Majes-ty's Empire?

"You seem surprised, Dr. Watson," she continued, "but at the end of *The Sign of Four,* when you found that the Agra treasure was irretrievably lost, you were overjoyed because there would be no barrier of wealth to stand between you and your future wife. And pray, how is Mrs. Watson?''

I apprised Miss Marx of my recent bereavement, and she seemed genuinely affected.

Meanwhile, Holmes was daring to ask Irene Adler some per-sonal questions. "May I inquire, Mrs. Norton, after the health of your husband?''

Irene Adler looked at Holmes directly. "We will shortly be divorced," she said. "I found that Mr. Norton and I shared little that was essential; an operatic singer does not blend too well in the company of English barristers, particularly if she is something of a socialist. I plan to begin a new career, Mr. Holmes.''

"And pray, Miss Adler, if I may address you thus by your ar-tistic name, what will be the nature of your career?''

"I plan to return to my native country, the United States. Did you know, Mr. Holmes, that I was born in New Jersey?''

"I believe I did, Miss Adler."

"A great migration is taking place to America, Mr. Holmes. Hundreds of thousands of Jews, Italians, and Poles are arriving in New York City every year. I should like to do for them what Arnold Toynbee has been doing here at the East End—to found what is called a 'settlement house' to help guide the immigrants in their new environment. Its purpose will be to teach them English, advise them as to employment, and help provide them with a cultural life—books, plays, opera, and dance. I speak their languages and know their original homelands. I shall help them become Americans, and I shall live among them."

"But are you not sacrificing your operatic career, Miss Adler?"

"I had already retired from the Warsaw Imperial Opera, Mr. Holmes, before I met the pompous potentate of Austria. Singing to amuse the bourgeois and aristocrats finally began to bore me. The more I saw those people prancing in their drawing rooms, the more socialistic I became. My cousin, Victor Adler, who leads a fledgling Austrian social democracy, urged me to call on Karl Marx, which I did; whereupon Eleanor Marx and I have been becoming friends. But I am so glad that you and I, Mr. Holmes, have met."

Irene Adler looked at Holmes with a certain intensity: "I hope, Mr. Holmes, you were drawn here this afternoon by the hope of meeting me."

Holmes flushed; I had never before seen his face suffused with color. "I had not been aware, Miss Adler," he said, "that you would be at the reading of an Ibsen play, but I must acknowledge that I an inordinately pleased that you are here."

I turned away to converse with Eleanor Marx, but she had left us and was much engaged with Bernard Shaw. Suddenly the booming voice of William Morris conquered the clamor, bidding everyone to find a seat on one of his lovely chairs, so that the reading of *A Doll's House* might shortly commence. I found myself reclining on an enormously comfortable sofa that made me feel like the Rajah of Nepal, and next to me was a young woman who looked to me like the loveliest of Indian beauties. When we introduced ourselves, she said she was May Morris, the daughter of our host; her tall, sinuous figure lent its curves to the shimmering green fabric of her dress, making her seem like an exotic tropical flower that might have kindled the imagination of a wandering explorer. I was almost dizzy with the impressions that were crowding upon me that afternoon. Never in my life had I been surrounded by so much beauty and brilliance. The truth or falsity of the ideas being propounded seemed altogether a secondary consideration; rather it was the comradeship that diffused the room in Kelmscott House, the sense of fellowship lived in the glorious search for a more beautiful and creative way of life. I felt myself in a sanctuary, privileged to glimpse for a few moments a harbinger of the future human society, and the image dazzled and confused me.

The readers meanwhile took their seats at the back of the room under the windows. Then the reading began. I was astonished to find how an unadorned recital of the play could so entrance me. As a medical student, I used to wander into the theater to sit far aloft in the balcony, straining to grasp all the meticulously hewn speech of the great Sir Henry Irving. I remember how I practically recited with him the always silencing soliloquy of Hamlet, and how I thrilled to the clank of the swords. But this Ibsen made drama of the lives and concerns of ordinary people such as I knew—their worries over debts, litigation, business. I have never liked women who repudiated their vocation for wifehood and motherhood, and have felt that they were properly the inspiration to men, the chief agency to elevate man from the bestial to the chivalrous. Yet I found that Eleanor Marx moved me so deeply as her character Nora evolved from submission to rebellion that at the end I was ready to applaud. Whether by choice or chance, the different readers were assigned roles that corresponded oddly to their characters. Edward Aveling read the part of Helmer, for whom a wife, despite all his professions of love, is but an instrument of pleasure and career; Shaw enacted Krogstad, the family friend whose guise conceals a would-be lover in a *ménage à trois*. The hours went by swiftly. From time to time, I glanced to the corner where Holmes and Irene sat together. He watched the play intently, and she sat with her features softened into a strange contentment. I wondered what drama's unspoken lines passed between them.

Then the enthusiastic applause sounded. Eleanor Marx was excited and vivacious as she received congratulations. I wished her well, and said I hoped that someday I would witness her performance on the stage. Then unexpectedly she asked Holmes and myself to dinner at her "Jews' Den," as she called her flat, for the coming Tuesday evening. Holmes and I agreed, and we left with warm goodbyes. At the doorstep, we encountered Irene Adler. To my surprise, Holmes asked whether an escort was seeing her home. She replied that she had none, that she had come alone, and that she lived at a Whitechapel settlement.

"In that case," asked Holmes, "would you allow me the pleasure of accompanying you?"

She took his arm very naturally. "We shall see each other later this evening, my dear Watson. I hope you shall not mind a solitary dinner."

I reassured him most sincerely on that score, and soon a hansom cab was driving them away. I stood on the pavement musing to myself when I became aware of Edward Aveling together with Eleanor Marx standing by my side. An unpleasant leer was affixed to Aveling's face. "Your friend Holmes," he said, "is as full of surprises as a child's jackanapes. He comes to listen to Ibsen, but he conquers a contralto."

I said nothing, but Eleanor chirped cheerfully: "We shall see you then Tuesday."

I bowed, as Aveling's face darkened. Evidently the invitation surprised him. Eleanor invited me to join their cab, but I responded that after so stimulating an afternoon I preferred to quiet my constitution with a walk along the Thames, its waves glowing in periodic reflection of the rising moon.

Homes returned to Baker Street late and gloomy. I tried to cheer him, saying again that certainly he had found out all he needed to bring the case of Eleanor Marx to a close; he could tell the facts to Frederick Engels, who would inform Karl Marx as to the details. Surely her family would be able to deal best with their daughter's mishap. They had brought her up on these newfangled socialist ideas of emancipation; it was theirs to resolve the domestic entanglement in which their daughter found herself.

Sherlock Holmes shook his head negatively. He began to speak: "When we reached the Whitechapel settlement house, Irene Adler found waiting for her a South African friend, a Miss Olive

Schreiner, who is writing a novel and is also a close personal friend of Miss Marx. Dr. Marx mentioned her name to us. Irene Adler and Olive Schreiner have been talking of Eleanor Marx for most of several weeks; Miss Schreiner talks readily of the most personal, intimate circumstances in Eleanor's life. I have never met two women who have adopted a standard of frankness in discourse otherwise more appropriate to medical volumes. Perhaps they have expressed their implicit confidence in me by speaking so frankly. Both agree that Eleanor Marx is high-strung and that she has had a difficult time trying to assert her own ambitions and longings against a father so domineering in person as Karl Marx. It is not only that she is in awe of him as the foremost man in the world's labor and socialist movements. She was Marx's child solace during the years when he was unknown, penurious, ridiculed, when the family was half-starved because Marx was penniless. A little brother died, little sisters died, the mother collapsed. Marx was himself like a helpless child when it came to earning his livelihood. Evidently, he made virtually no effort to secure regular employment, and bantered that he failed to obtain a position as railway clerk because his handwriting was so bad. I have generally found that educated men with willfully bad handwritings have dictatorial, perverse dispositions. Marx fortunately was invited to become the European correspondent for an American socialist newspaper, the *New York Tribune*. It's no longer a socialist paper, and in fact, I find its journalistic accounts of criminal cases excellent, if a bit more lurid than our *Daily Telegraph*. At any rate, the *Tribune* paid Marx well, and Eleanor Marx has a warm gratitude toward Americans. Meanwhile, for years, she comforted her father, idolized him, read poetry to him—Shakespeare, Walter Scott, even the melancholy Thomson of the *City of Dreadful Night*.

"Do you refer, Holmes, to that gloomy, suicidal poem that has recently had a certain vogue? Marx spoke of it, too."

"Yes, my dear Watson, a poem on the sheer horror of existence, and the escape through chosen death."

"I rather regret that Eleanor Marx likes that sort of poetry. I have often suspected that the kind of poetry a person likes is the best indicator of his fortitude; I deplore an attraction to suicidal verse. But, pray, continue your narrative, Holmes."

"A few months ago, Eleanor Marx encountered Edward Aveling. They met at readings of the Shelley Society. Aveling read the poems with feeling, and talked of the transforming power of love. He also spoke of the union of science and love; he told how he, as a zoologist, was filled with a pantheistic adoration as he contemplated the vast epic of evolution, the countless varieties of creatures, and the emergence of man. She read his articles in the *National Reformer,* a long series in which he brilliantly traced the evolution of Darwin's theories through his lifetime of scientific writings. Probably this penniless man, a doctor of science with no position in the university world, filled with social idealism and making his uncertain living as a journalist, reminded Eleanor Marx of her father. Her friends agree that she fell in love with this man completely and hopelessly, feeling as certain as one could be that there would be no other man in her life.

"Both Irene Adler and Olive Schreiner had heard dark rumors of this man. They knew he had a living wife. But Eleanor assured them she knew that whole story, that Mrs. Aveling was a wealthy woman who refused to live with a husband who professed such heterodox ideas. They had heard of transient relationships in which he had cruelly misused several women, and even sunk to extracting from them liberal financial gifts. To which Eleanor Marx replied that his is a warm, ardent temperament, anxious to give himself to the lonely in spirit, and that the monies he received were always allocated to the Freethought Movement. Her own father, she said, had also lived for many years from the largesse of friends, and ugly rumors were also spread in his case that he was engaged in self-enrichment. Aveling in her view lived as abstemiously as her father had.

"In short, Eleanor Marx felt herself unshakably joined to Edward Aveling.

"Then one evening at Engels's house, an episode occurred that shook the foundations of Eleanor's mental life. There had been some unpleasant words with her mother and father concerning her acting ambitions, but no more than usual. Eleanor walked to Engels's residence to enjoy some relaxation, singing, and good conversation. To her surprise the Marxes' lifetime house-servant, Lenchen, was there, and with her, a young man. Engels and Lenchen both seemed somewhat ill at ease. Then Lenchen said to Eleanor, 'I wish to present to you my son, Freddie, Frederick Demuth.'

"Eleanor Marx was astonished. 'But you never told me you had a son, Lenchen dear, and such a fine young man.' And Freddie, dressed in simple clothes, a workingman with only a few years' schooling, seemed indeed a straightforward, intelligent, kindly young man. Engels kept hovering over them all, and Eleanor was puzzled at the way in which Freddie evidently looked to him for authority. The evening went by pleasantly enough, with Engels doing his rendition of 'The Vicar of Bray' and his political peregrinations.

"When Eleanor Marx returned home, her father was still awake, studying Russian grammar; her mother was asleep. Eleanor naturally bubbled at once with her gossip; she had been to the General's house and had met a young man, Freddie, who was Lenchen's son. Had he known that Lenchen had a son? Karl Marx seemed visibly upset. He said something about having known about it. He said, 'Don't tell your mother you met Freddie. She gets angry with Engels when she hears about him.' Eleanor Marx at once inferred that Engels was probably the father of young Freddie. Karl Marx had not exactly said so, but his words were open to that construction. Eleanor was flustered, but said nothing, and retired to her room after kissing her father good night.

"As she prepared herself for bed, she glanced at her mantelpiece, where stood a daguerreotype of her father as a young man. Suddenly she began to shake. The face of Karl Marx as a student at Berlin was almost the duplicate of that of the young workingman, Freddie Demuth. A profound fear seized her, a terrible, dark suspicion. Perhaps that suspicion would not have crossed her mind had Eleanor not been immersed in the translating of Ibsen's plays. Evidently the theme of the illegitimate child, born of a servant girl and the master of the house, is not absent from them; nor the dubious role of the family friend throughout the intrigue. Was such a suspicion, Eleanor asked herself, the perverse outcome of her Ibsenite enthusiasm? Was she transforming her own home into a stage for characters out of Ibsen pursuing their tragic inevitabilities?

"But the resemblance between the young Karl Marx and the

young Freddie Demuth was an emphatic diagram for the corollary she feared to draw. And why should her mother object to having this child of dear Lenchen enter the house? Freddie, to be sure, was just a young workingman, but he was decent and honest and a far better person than some of the pompous workingmen's leaders who occasionally visited their house, and whom Karl Marx derided for having sold their souls to the Liberals in exchange for promises of parliamentary candidacies. But if her own father was the father of Freddie, then during all these years what a horrible partition must have divided her father and mother! Surely Momma must have observed Lenchen's pregnancy day by day.

"Now Eleanor perceived that her father's remark had intimated that because Engels was the father of the child, that therefore Mrs. Marx was angry with him. Could it be, however, that Marx feared to have Freddie Demuth enter their house lest his wife see before her own eyes the eloquent image in the illegitimate child of her own youthful Karl? The shock might indeed destroy Jenny von Westphalen Marx; her previous nervous collapses would culminate in a final unhinging of her mind under the impact of a tawdry testimony of personal disloyalty. Had a hypocrisy more elemental than bourgeois been pervading their lives? Had the half-brother, minister of the interior to the king of Prussia and chief of Bismarck's secret police, been right in warning her mother not to marry this Jewish adventurer who repudiated Christian morality as a Jewish commercial excrescence? Better to die than to think that one's idealism was the garment of simple stupidity. Eleanor Marx sat down on her bed stunned.

"As time went on, she could not speak; she could not eat. She could not bring herself to look at the eyes of her mother and father. She sat listlessly. Her father rushed to his young friend, the professor of zoology, Edwin Ray Lankester, who quickly brought Dr. Donkin to the house. He found Eleanor's stomach completely deranged and significantly, too, there were the nervous symptoms of a facial tic, a trembling of the hands, and convulsive spasms. Eleanor, by refusing to eat, was presumably punishing herself, in the way so many persons afflicted with mental and nervous disturbances do. Dr. Donkin tried, by questioning Eleanor, to ascertain whether she had been severely tried by any recent, upsetting occurrence. Eleanor Marx looked at him vacantly with her luminous, now staring eyes. Dr. Donkin advised Marx to allow his daughter to spend much time with her friends. The old revolutionist was crestfallen. He could no longer delight his daughter by telling her the long, endless stories that used to entrance her. Those interminable adventures were now terminated.

"The next day Eleanor Marx rose. She said she was going to the British Museum Library and might attend a reading in the evening with Bernard Shaw and another friend. She went to the British Museum. There she met Edward Aveling. He saw her—weak, shattered, apathetic, vulnerable—and asked her to come live with him, to merge their misfortunes, and, together defying society and its conventions, to build their own happiness based on a pure love and a common ideal. Eleanor knew that her father would countenance no intimacy or even close friendship with a man already legally married. She had seen the anger and contempt that lined Marx's forehead and face when he spoke of silly women who gave themselves to adventurers. She had seen him watching over his daughters' suitors, inquiring into their family backgrounds and fortunes and questioning them as to their professional prospects. Marx's political philosophy speaks most sincerely not in the pamphlets written to build a political movement and reputation or in the epigrams he fashioned to win the admiration of his fellow doctors of philosophy. No, it expressed itself most honestly when he acted to safeguard his children's welfare. And at this point Marx threw aside all his youthful encomia of the free sexual love that would overcome the separation of the spirit from the body that the parsons had inflicted on human beings. Eleanor Marx knew thoroughly her father's feelings. Overwhelmed, however, and in despair from the stupefying discovery that exposed the chief pillar of her existence as crumbling clay, Eleanor Marx, in an act of supreme defiance, accepted Edward Aveling as her chosen one and together they walked to his rooms at Russell Street.

"There is little further to add, my dear Watson, to this tragic story of father and daughter. Our Ibsenite reader is an Ibsenite tragedian, with a supporting cast of characters each of whom is likewise an agent or cooperating supernumerary in the drama of inescapable defeat. Miss Olive Schreiner says that Aveling reminds her of the shadows that appear in the evening on the African veld. They seem to give forth effluvia of evil; if they envelope the individual, he is doomed, because he has breathed and absorbed evil into his marrow. The Kaffirs flee and wait for the sunshine to dispel the henchmen of darkness; no spells will be of any avail against evil unalloyed. But Miss Schreiner speaks with that exaggeration allowable only to writers of fiction.

"I, on the other hand, my dear Watson, have been retained by Friedrich Engels and Karl Marx to return the prodigal daughter to the father's house, and I mean to do so within three days."

The hour was late. I felt singularly moved by the narrative of Sherlock Holmes, and I surmised that my friend's emotions had become more involved in this case than I had ever seen happen before.

"Holmes," I cried. "I am a physician, and we learn at the hospital that our judgment will inevitably go astray if we allow our emotions to become involved with the health or survival of our patients. It is the sad imperative of our profession that, to think clearly about a person's illness, we must disregard his character, his unique mixture of good and evil, and think of him as the resultant of physicochemical forces and interactions. Afterwards, we can allow ourselves the leavening pleasure of regarding him as a soul. And you as a detective, I beg humble leave to say, are a kind of social physician, a social diagnostician, retained to study some social infection and to invoke the lancet of the law when necessary. But, I fear, now that you have accomplished your social diagnosis, there is little more you can do. Eleanor Marx is of age, and she is at liberty, according to the law, to cohabit with whomsoever she chooses. You can inform Messrs. Engels and Marx of her whereabouts and her choice. But there is nothing more you can do. I half feel, my dear Holmes, that if our laws had not abolished dueling, you would be standing tomorrow at dawn, pistol in hand, to exchange shots with Edward B. Aveling. I am rather glad, my dear Holmes, that that will not be the case. I should find the anxiety of serving as your second more enervating than the impact of the Jezail bullet in the Afghan ambush, and I should hate to see you risk your life, so useful to society, for the sake of a hysterical girl, brought up by a domestic tyrant whose despicable conduct and hypocritical principles are making a sacrifice of his daughter. Karl Marx reminds me of the half-savage Jephthah, who immolated his daughter to the semi-savage volcanic god Yahweh."

"Your biblical erudition, my dear Watson, sometimes astounds me. I must confess that I have done little reading in the Scriptures and am wholly ignorant as to the provenance of Jephthah."

"Jephthah, my dear Holmes," I said, "is the name of a famous Hebrew warrior who appears in the Book of Judges, and whose sacrifice of his daughter was akin to that in the legend of Agamemnon told by the Greeks. And I know only as much of the Bible as a child attending Sunday school classes would learn at chapel or kirk."

"Neither of which institutions, my dear Watson, I enjoyed. My father was a disciple of John Stuart Mill and lived by the utilitarian philosophy. My mother was advised to emulate Harriet Taylor and George Eliot. I was early set to reading Mill's *Logic,* and his methods of induction I promptly assimilated into my own science of deduction."

"But how did you develop your tremendous interest in crime, Holmes?"

"As far as I can remember, Watson, it began in 1865 when I was a growing boy. My father as a Millite was a staunch supporter of the North in the American Civil War, and as warm a partisan of Abraham Lincoln as ever was. He attended meetings sympathetic to the Union cause, and deemed the Confederates to be allies of the devil. Then Lincoln was assassinated by a young Shakespearean actor, John Wilkes Booth. My father condemned Booth bitterly, and thought no punishment too severe for the conspirators. I, on the contrary, asked, in Millite terms, whether social circumstances hadn't shaped the assassin's mind and whether perhaps his Shakespearean acting as Brutus, a murderer of Caesar but albeit 'the noblest Roman of the all,' hadn't affected his mind. My father was rather annoyed, and I found myself henceforth much interested in the characters and deeds of criminals. And slowly I have arrived at the opinion that there is an irreducible constituent in our characters that is not the outcome of social circumstances but which, within limits, chooses among the circumstances those that will most affect us. But we are losing ourselves in metaphysics, and I must remember an arduous day awaits me on the morrow."

Chapter Four

The next morning Holmes was once more gone before I arose, and he did not reappear until long after dinner. For a moment, as the door opened, and he entered, I did not recognize him. His complexion was darkened, his hair wild and unkempt, his face mustached, and his clothes were like those of a dock-worker, with two sweaters and a cap poised at a threatening angle.

"Holmes," I expostulated, "what have you been about?"

"There is something primordial in our character, my dear Watson, that pursuing a man evokes. Man's distant ancestors, according to Charles Darwin's *The Descent of Man,* were hunters and used clubs, stones, arrows, and spears to kill animals and fish. To track one's prey in the forest, to sit for hours quietly at a watering place waiting for the animal one seeks—those were the experiences that selected our forebears to be the survivors of their bands. All day I have been tracking Edward Aveling. It has been sickening. I have been led from the offices of the *National Reformer,* the organ of the self-righteous secularists, to haunts of depravities that are literally unspeakable. What I have learned of Edward B. Aveling would qualify him for inclusion in the pages of some medical casebook, where deeds that exceed the tolerance of the English language can be clothed in the obscurity of Latin idioms.

"I watched by the tumbledown, two-story tenement in Stonecutter Street, just off Shoe Lane, that provides the headquarters for the Freethought Publishing Company. Aveling came by at nine o'clock. I lolled around at a public house across the street, melting in with the joyless jobless at their entertainments. I gathered quickly that they had no high opinion of the freethinkers; they thought it should be renamed the Freelove Publishing Company and they claimed that the old M.P., Bradlaugh, and the young doctor with the stoop, Aveling, were in a competition for the favors of the buxom Mrs. Annie Besant, who, they say, was so notorious for keeping a bordello of lovers that every court in the land had judged her an unfit mother and deprived her of her two children. 'They tell in their papers they're republican, atheistic, and Malthusian; I say they're anarchist, free lover, and child-hating. I could speak a thing or two about the doctor and little girls,' said one jiber. 'They lecture at the Hall of Science. Ridiculous playactors. Newton and Faraday would have had no use for the likes of them.'

"Luncheon time came, and I sat and ate a dish of fish and chips with the lads. Suddenly, I spied Aveling leaving the house. I arose, waved my farewell, and was off, following Aveling at a decent distance. A few streets away, he paused and entered an unoccupied house. A few minutes later he emerged, looking, to my surprise, somewhat altered. A green cap had replaced the hat that was evidently now in his small briefcase. A mustache was attached to his face, and his complexion darkened. He proceeded rapidly for about ten minutes, then turned into an alley where there was a ramshackle, poorly lighted inn, the Nell Gwynn, as it announced itself in half-erased red letters.

"Aveling entered, and I soon after. The riffraff of the docks sat about talking—desperate, cheerless men, Swedes, Lascars, Burmese, Chinese, and several women—trying to maintain a superficial camaraderie that poorly concealed an inner hatred for all and sundry. Aveling evidently had disappeared upstairs into some room. I sat watching, conjecturing. About a half-hour later, Aveling stepped from a room that I could see on the balcony, came down, saluted the innkeeper, tossed him some money, and left. I remained waiting. A few minutes later a young girl—a child—innocent looking yet with a bewildered expression, appeared from the same room, descended, and left. Nobody seemed to notice.

"I ambled over to the bar and asked for some bitters. The innkeeper looked at me and growled: 'Some folks have strange ways.

72

That's 'un I hate to see. But he pays his money, and there's a lot of young children about here ready to do anything to help their mothers, brothers, and sisters. Usually there ain't no father around.'

"I muttered something to the effect that the man looked like an 'eddicated bloke.'

" 'Eddication, eddication,' snarled the innkeeper, 'they're just as rotten after they've stuffed their head with books as they were before. Taking that poor Jennie Burns. She looked fit to die when she left. But she lives right around the corner on Thompson Street and doesn't have more than a few steps to walk. I ain't seen you here before.'

" 'No, just came down yesterday from Manchester. The mills are slack,' I told him.

" 'Hope you find a job soon,' he said.

"I left the Nell Gwynn and walked around the corner on Thompson Street. Little Jennie Burns was sitting on the stairs in front of a small tenement in which she presumably lived. 'Hello, Jennie,' I said. 'I saw you at the Nell Gwynn.'

"The child looked at me with eyes that were immensely sad. 'I've begun to work there,' she said, 'for such gentlemen as may want me.'

"In the course of my work, Watson, I have encountered horrors of all kinds, cruelties, hatreds, greeds; I have met victims, men and women, of treachery, murder, dishonesty. But never in all the years, Watson, have I met a victim who so affected me by the depth of her misery, bottomless, inexplicable.

" 'What kind of work does your father do, Jennie?' I asked.

" 'My father died two years ago. He was a carpenter. My mother sews and mends clothes. I'm the oldest of the four children. I used to take care of them, but my mother doesn't earn enough, so I have to help out. The gentlemen pay more than I could make at a factory. I try then to forget about them.'

" 'Do they come back to the Nell Gwynn for you, Jennie?'

" 'Only sometimes. The last gentleman I saw today returns every two weeks at about the same time. He likes to talk long words that I don't understand. Sometimes, however, he's grouchy, and says not a word. Another time he recited a poem. He hurried the words, and I couldn't understand them. I asked him what they said. He answered: "Better to die." But he pays me well. Once he said: "You're the only one I pay on time." A very odd gentleman.'

"I gave her a shilling, Watson, and bade her buy milk, cheese, and bread for her family. She thanked me profusely."

I listened to Holmes's narrative, scarcely knowing what to reply. Better to embattle murderers in quest of jewels, thieves wreaking vengeance on a turncoat, or even blackmailers extorting monies from men and women fearful of their own pasts. But how could one measure the inhuman villainy of a man who misused the innocence of a child? I felt ashamed that the great kingdom that I had served, the imperial power whose soldier I was proud to be, allowed such misery to thrive like a fungus in the dark alleys of its greatest city.

Meanwhile, I looked forward to dinner at the "Jews' Den" of Eleanor Marx and Edward Aveling with apprehension. A spirit of self-destruction seemed to hover about her, even as one of evil permeated her consort. Why, I asked myself, should this young woman raised in surroundings of the highest culture be attracted to an agent of evil? I mused over the strange polarities in life, and lost myself in a quagmire of unanswerable questions. I found myself uneasy in the atmosphere that pervaded the London community of the young intellectual adventurers. I had a sense of people living on the borders of the irrational, and I almost longed for a return to the familiar commonplace motives of greed, revenge, and power that characterized the thieves, swindlers, and murderers of Holmes's usual cases. At least they did not bedeck themselves with philosophies and something of which I had never heard before, "ideology."

Holmes disappeared the next day until an hour or so before dinner; then, after dressing with a care I had not hitherto observed in him, we drove off to Russell Street. Eleanor Marx herself opened the door and welcomed us into their rooms. Their main one, used obviously for dinner and discussion, was of moderate proportions; its walls were adorned with an assortment of literary portraits. Holmes bemusedly read their names aloud: "Shakespeare, Shelley, Byron, Walter Scott, but where Miss Marx, are Wordsworth, Coleridge, and Daniel Defoe?"

"Mr. Holmes, we reverence those who remained loyal to the people's cause, as did Shelley and Byron, but we have small respect for Wordsworth and Coleridge, who betrayed the revolution they had loved in their youth."

"Yet Shakespeare, Miss Marx, scarcely admired the working classes. I recall that his mobs of Roman proletarians were unthinking, volatile, and ready to join in violence with the unworthiest demagogue."

"Shakespeare, Mr. Holmes, transcends all rules of politics and aesthetics alike. He belonged to the people despite himself. He aimed to make Shylock a ridiculous, bloodthirsty buffoon, but instead gave him such wondrous lines that Shylock became the most eloquent spokesman for human equality that has ever trod the foot boards. Caesar portends the world's social organization even as Brutus represents the counterpart principle of freedom. Ours is the social democratic task of unifying both principles hitherto at war, to realize the human aspirations that have until now wasted themselves in tragedy."

Edward Aveling now joined us from a side door. We were introduced to two other guests, both very young, a Miss Amy Levy and a Mr. Israel Zangwill. He was a gangling, still adolescent youth, with a very Oriental face—olive-skinned, high cheek-boned, and thick-lipped.

"You see, Mr. Holmes, that tonight you and Dr. Watson will really be dining at a 'Jews' Den.' Amy Levy will one day be our greatest poetess and Israel Zangwill our greatest novelist."

Throughout all of Eleanor Marx's vivacious and exuberant conversation, Edward Aveling seemed to be standing good-naturedly aloof. I sensed that Aveling was on guard against Holmes, and felt that he was being observed, as if his terrain were being reconnoitered by an enemy intending some undefined blow. And I almost felt, too, that this charming scientific villain was meditating his counteroffensive, that perhaps he would not stop short of trying to annihilate Holmes and render him as extinct in the evolutionary sequence as those curious species upon whose fossils he discoursed.

We all then followed our hostess to seats around a small table, where she served us several unusual dishes that Holmes seemed to relish very much. "I find the fish dish most enjoyable, Miss Marx," said Holmes. "Pray, what exactly is it?"

"I shall tell you," she replied, "provided that you call me Mrs. Aveling."

Holmes paused for a moment as Aveling observed his hesitation closely. "Do you hesitate, Mr. Holmes," he said with a slight sarcasm, "to recognize that a free union made with the affection of its participants is as valid as those warranted for loveless couples by legal documents?"

Holmes replied: "By whatever name you choose to be known, Mrs. Aveling, your qualities of sincerity, intelligence, and generosity will be attested by all."

Eleanor Marx looked pleased. "This dish, Mr. Holmes, is a traditional Jewish one known as 'gefilte fish.' It consists of chopped carp and whitefish ground up and mixed with bread, egg, onion, and pepper and then cooked with onions. The red spicing is made of beets and radishes. And the rye bread comes from a Polish-Jewish bakery."

I have never seen Holmes enjoy food so much; he became somewhat more loquacious with the company than I had previously seen. He told Amy Levy and Eleanor Marx that he had never studied national diets, that he realized now this was a deficiency he must remedy. He was delighted by a chicken soup with noodles and a delicious serving of roast chicken.

"Amy," said Eleanor Marx, "kindly taught me how to cook these dishes. Her mother came from Poland and knows all the traditional recipes. I had known nothing of them. I am the only one in my family to have an attachment to the traditional Jewish customs."

"And pray, Miss Levy," said Holmes, "in what sort of work are you engaged?"

Amy Levy looked at Holmes gravely with her black eyes, which seemed too large for her delicate features. Her olive skin was marked by no bright color and her black hair was combed back to a simple conjuncture; her eyes seemed to punctuate the sadness of things and her smiles were like sparks of freedom that her melancholy could not smother.

"I have just spent two years at Cambridge," she said, "at

Newnham College; several poems of mine have been published in the *Pelican* and the *Cambridge Review.*"

Holmes answered that he had not seen these journals.

"Now," said Amy Levy, "I am writing a longish poem, 'Xantippe,' in defense of that much abused and long-suffering wife of Socrates."

"A most unusual and original theme," said Holmes.

"It begins," said Amy Levy, "with the feelings of young Xantippe at the age of seventeen, her revulsion against the aged, ugly metaphysician to whom she is being wedded. Then the poem depicts her awakening to the fact that she is scarcely regarded as a rational being by this adulated philosopher."

"I think many an Oxonian, bred at Balliol College under Principal Jowett will cavil at your poem, Miss Levy."

Amy Levy looked stern: "My Xantippe will speak for women despised in marriage by their husbands:

> ". . . hope died out;
> "A huge despair was stealing on my soul,
> "A sort of fierce acceptance of my fate,
> "He wished a household vessel . . ."

Eleanor Marx interrupted: "Amy is a prophetess of the future woman; she is the poetess of the new feminism. Surely you must have heard of this new movement, Mr. Holmes. It is trying to realize all that the noble John Stuart Mill proposed in that irrefutable masterpiece of his, *The Subjection of Women.* Have you read it, Mr. Holmes?"

"No, Miss Marx, I have not read Mill's works, apart from his *Logic,* which interested me in my professional capacity."

"Well, you must learn of the feminist movement. The best way to begin would be to listen to the lectures on the matriarchate and the place of women in civilization that Karl Pearson is giving at the South Place Church. He is a brilliant mathematician, a lawyer, and a scholar with a learning that ranges from Maimonides to Clerk Maxwell. He proves beyond any reasonable doubt that the chief advances in prehistoric times that created the foundation for civilized life were accomplished by women."

"That is a thesis which I would not contest, Miss Marx. After all, as my good friend Dr. Watson will someday inform the public, your friend Miss Irene Adler is the only person who, in all my practice, ever completely and decisively foiled my best efforts."

"Irene is wonderful, Mr. Holmes."

Edward Aveling looked uncomfortable.

Eleanor Marx added teasingly: "Irene Adler is among the few women of London's intellectual circle who have been impervious to Edward's fascination."

Holmes turned to Amy Levy again. "Have you ever thought, Miss Levy, of writing a novel about London's intellectual world? My brief acquaintance with it makes me think that an artist would find his or her powers fully evoked in its portraiture."

"I do plan to write a novel, Mr. Holmes, after I have completed my 'Xantippe.' But it will be a novel of the Jews I have known, young and old, and their problems of character, their formations, indeed their deformations, as they try to commingle with British society."

"I should think, Miss Levy, that would be a very painful novel to write, probing into the personal conflicts of those one loves best."

"I shall indeed," said Amy Levy, "indict my own people. For theirs has become a religion of materialism; regrettably the Jews have accepted this materialistic age unqualifiedly, and have become materialists to their very fingertips."

"That is not so," said Eleanor Marx vehemently. "I have gone among the Jewish tailors in the East End trying to organize them into a trade union. I have never met a finer, more idealistic group of men; they live poor in body, but they are rich in spirit."

Amy Levy smiled sadly: "Dear Eleanor," she said, "grew up without a trace of Judaic religion or customs in her family's life. She is part German, part Scot, and part Jew. But I am a child of Jewry. Let me tell you that every Jewish young man I know is affected by nervous disorder. Every one of them I met at the university feels himself existing in a vulnerable, unstable equilibrium, a mixture composed of nomadic superstitions, outworn theologies and rituals, the insecurity and matching greed of one's elders, a striving for power and the realization of its vanity, and an attraction to secular science and learning. They feel themselves drawn to philosophies of despair, to Schopenhauer, or to nihilism, with its search for a suicide sanctified by a political gospel."

"You are wrong, Amy, about the terrorists; they are noble-hearted idealists," said Eleanor Marx.

"I have met them too," said Amy Levy. "I have talked for long hours with Leo Hartmann, the emissary of the Russian People's Will and its martyred assassins, and with Sergius Stepniak, the killer of General Trepov. Believe me, dear Eleanor, these terrorists are impelled to self-destruction like moths drawn to a candle-flame. They choose suicidal means because suicide is their unspoken end. An inner misery, intractable and irremediable, decrees their role as political tragedians. That is why the Jews are so numerous among the Nihilists even though the Nihilists applaud the peasants' pogroms."

"That cannot be," said Eleanor Marx excitedly. "The terrorists are high-minded altruists. You should have heard all Hartmann told us when he stayed at our home about the saintly Sofia Perovskaya, the daughter of the governor general of Moscow, who sacrificed her life of comfort to assassinate the Czar."

"And that same Hartmann tried to seduce you at your home, and 'Pumps,' the niece, at Engels's house," said Amy with a calm sadness.

Eleanor Marx blushed. "One cannot attach much importance," she said, "to the sexual moods of men and women living at the edge of death."

"Surely, however, Miss Levy," said Holmes, "what you say of death-seeking Russians has very little significance in our British environment, where common sense rules. It is more than two hundred years since any Englishman plotted to assassinate the king or queen or the first minister. Russia is still a medieval land, and we should hardly turn to it for lessons in either science, philosophy, or politics. And I am quite surprised that you dwell so much on what you judge to be the nervous dispositions of gifted Jews. Only a year has passed since the death of the Earl of Beaconsfield. Was ever a statesman more imperturbable and more endowed with a cheerful humor than Mr. Benjamin Disraeli? The British people, like their queen, were certain that his hands would not falter, nor his judgment waver, when he held the helm of our state. He was the least self-destructive of men."

Amy Levy responded that she had in mind the children of the recent generation of Polish- and Russian-Jewish immigrants. They were bred to a Jewish culture that one of Italian extraction such as Disraeli was happily spared.

"Someday I shall write a novel," said Amy, "in which I follow a young Jew from his Orthodox family to Oxford, the Inns of Court, and the House of Commons. You will not find it a gracious story like the career of Lord Rothschild, nor will it make of every educated Jew a virtual Spinoza, as George Eliot overgenerously tended to do in *Daniel Deronda*. Perhaps, however, our young friend, Mr. Zangwill, who knows more about the Ghetto than I ever shall, will write its untold story."

Mr. Israel Zangwill smiled with a youthful spontaneity. "I think, Amy," he said, "that you allow one or two instances of disturbed young men to impress you too much. The Oxford life of scholarly celibacy is a novel situation for a people whose young men and women were until recently married in their youth. We are adapting to novel customs and novel ideas, but on the whole we have made the leap from prefeudal to modern ideas very well. Above all, we have retained our sense of humor; Yiddish humor has always leveled the mighty and the maimed, and reminded God that He chose us, but for what? I am now even trying to persuade Eleanor to collaborate with me on a satire of *A Doll's House*. Imagine Nora a few years after her dolldom is over; she would realize that her own weak character had much to do with shaping the characters of her husband and family, and that her Bohemian existence was even more a doll's indulgence."

Edward Aveling had throughout the discussion sat with a condescending expression. Now he turned upon Amy Levy, and said: "My dear Amy, your poetry and your fiction would change overnight if you would allow yourself to fall in love and know the joys of womanhood. All your lamentations over the Jewish people would become as obsolete as the jeremiads of Jeremiah himself if you allowed yourself the normal biological fulfillment of sexual joy. Then you would write not of a ridiculous Xantippe but about a lustrous Diotima and her teachings of love to Socrates. Your melancholy would dissolve, and your eyes would shine. The Amy in your nature must triumph over the Levy, the lover over the Levite.''

Amy Levy sat as if numbed, like a wounded bird. Holmes looked at Aveling with cold, hostile eyes and tensed arms so that I thought for a moment he was preparing to strike the doctor of science. I had never before heard a man address a woman so and discuss her thoughts as if there were naught in her of the spiritual being but only the desirer and the desired of sexual utility. Was this then the outcome of the study of zoological evolution? Was this then the consequence of the principles of Charles Darwin applied to morality?

Amy Levy rose abruptly. She was leaving, she said. Aveling regarded her with an angular, malicious half-smirk on his face; Eleanor Marx looked embarrassed, distraught, and unhappy. Mr. Israel Zangwill was attentive, as though recording the scene for a future novel.

Holmes rose, and addressing Amy gallantly asked: "Might Dr. Watson and I have the honor, Miss Levy, of escorting you to your home?"

Amy Levy nodded her consent. We left almost formally. Holmes and I thanked Eleanor Marx warmly for her hospitality, and she said plaintively that she would be at the British Museum Reading Room every afternoon for the next week and hoped she and Holmes might talk in the surroundings of books. We bowed to Dr. Aveling and left.

Chapter Five

s the hansom cab drove us to Bloomsbury, where Amy Levy lived with her family, she remarked that having lived there all her years, she knew nothing of life in the woods and fields. I suggested to her that, as a medical man, I would well advise her to quit the harried city for a long while and not return until her cheeks glowed with the reflection of sunshine. "The joy of life would awaken in you," I said, "if you sojourned among simpler living things." She laughed lightly, and as she stepped from the cab, awaited by Holmes and myself, she burst into bitter tears. Holmes tried gently to console her, saying how much he had enjoyed her words that evening and that she should pay no heed to the malicious remarks of a scoundrel. The uncommon force of Holmes's statement seemed to comfort her; indeed, she seemed surprised but also pleased to hear Holmes describe Edward Aveling as a "scoundrel." She shook our hands warmly, thanked Holmes with deep sincerity, and climbed the stairs to her door. Holmes, looking very downcast, said nothing till we were seated beside a blazing, animated fire in our Baker Street lodgings.

"I have had very little occasion, Watson, apart from a few professional encounters, to meet with Jews. I did once listen to several mathematical lectures given by a great Jewish professor, Sylvester; he was the most exuberant, enthusiastic teacher I have ever known, and he seemed to revel in every algebraic equation as a poem that gave insight into some distinctive aspect of reality.

"But I have never been among a gathering of Jews, and tonight I was struck by a sense of fatality, of an inevitable ominous outcome, that weighs on their young. Or perhaps Eleanor Marx and Amy Levy are exceptions. They have taken difficult paths as

HOLMES SAID NOTHING TILL WE WERE SEATED BESIDE A BLAZING FIRE.

women. I do not think either of their lives will be happy. The nightmare that modern ideas have brought to so many intelligent persons—wasn't that Huxley's phrase—seems to have descended heavily upon both young women. Perhaps they would have been far happier if they had accepted the support of their religious traditions. Do you remember the pages in *The Descent of Man* on the evolution of the moral and social senses? The solitary negation of ties would scarcely have helped man to survive in the struggle for existence. Tomorrow I shall try to speak reasonable words to Eleanor Marx.''

The following day Holmes was gone once again before I was ready for breakfast. He returned in the late afternoon looking downcast and sought to alleviate his gloom by narrating his experiences.

"The British Museum Library," he began, "deserves to be ranked together with the ancient library of Alexandria for its contribution to civilization. It is the real headquarters of the world's social and scientific movement. The spectacle of the of the rows of heads, young and old, bent over mathematical books, governmental reports, tattered newspapers, and yellowed manuscripts is awesome. Mr. Shaw this morning showed me the table and seat at which Karl Marx wrote *Das Kapital*. He said a great plaque should be constructed at this table with the inscription: 'At this desk Karl Marx toiled through poverty and privation to demonstrate the law of the inevitable decline of capitalist civilization and its supersession by a new socialist world more glorious for the spirit of man!' Then he thrust the latest issue of *The Fortnightly* into my hands, saying: 'Read the article by Professor Robert O. Moriarty, "Crime in the Twentieth Century." He and Edward Aveling are inseparable friends, and this is the first Marxist article on crime that I have ever read.'

"I proceeded to read the essay, and believe me, Watson, it is the most original sociological theory of crime I have ever seen; but it fills me with fear and foreboding for the endurance of our civilization. Moriarty says that he is applying Marx's method, so that from the nature of economic developments, he can forecast the future evolution of crime. Our bourgeois society, he claims, is breaking up, decaying from within, dissolving. Under such circumstances, he claims, the criminal becomes the ideal type of revolutionist. Moriarty says that he is synthesizing the ideas of a Russian anarchist communist, Michael Bakunin, with those of Marx. Bakunin claimed that the brigand is the highest example of the practicing revolutionist. The brigand does not sit in a library, but each criminal act of his is a revolutionary act. He directly expropriates the capitalists, the bourgeoisie, the landlords, and thus, by revolutionary deed, nullifies the laws of property and discredits the bourgeois system in the eyes of the masses. Our system is shown to be weak and ineffectual; when its police officers try to capture the brigands, the policemen themselves are assassinated, terrorized, intimidated, subdued, bribed, corrupted. The whole society begins to reek with the fume of decay, even as the Roman Empire in its decline was brought low by endemic brigandage, thievery, and lawlessness.

"But Professor Moriarty argues further that crime in the twentieth century will take new forms, reflecting the emerging structure of centralized capitalism. He quotes a long paragraph from a book by our friend Engels; the 'anarchy of production,' it says, that is, the petty bourgeois system of competing factories, is being replaced by an organized system of monopolies. Production becomes centralized as the more efficient enterprises absorb or survive triumphantly among their rivals. And correspondingly, says Professor Moriarty, the system of petty bourgeois crime that has flourished hitherto is destined to pass away. The individually acting criminal belongs to the petty bourgeois stage of production: 'Its returns were small, and its physical risks were always great.' The new order of crime will be as centralized as a modern monopoly, efficient and economical. The escapes of malefactors will be organized by cooperative teams and alibis will be fashioned with a trained group of witnesses. Counsel, permanently retained, will always be available for circumventing justice. Centralized criminal agencies will extract tribute from industrial enterprises and banks in exchange for the criminals' promises not to rob, engage in 'sabotage,' as they now say, or steal. And as the socialist society takes shape, the criminal class, organized as a criminal college or corporation, will provide the society's dominant coercive force. It will eradicate recalcitrant critics and permeate all strata with its network of criminal informers; the Roman organization survived not only because its legions stood guard on the frontiers but also because a huge corps of informers watched over the people and eliminated doubters, dissenters, and dreamers. The criminal class is the only one completely exempt from bourgeois morality; it will provide the socialist Machiavellians. Let the literary men, the poets, politicians, and agitators play their parts as socialist Savonarolas. They will end as he did, executed, while the criminal class takes power as the agency for socialist control.

"This Professor Moriarty is immensely learned. He maintains

that all history shows that the advance of mankind is due not to the law-abiding but to the lawbreakers. The first political states, he says, were created by criminals who extorted tribute from the underlying population; now we call tributes 'taxes.' The lords are the descendants of criminal extortioners. Genghis Khan was a criminal on a grandiose scale. The Roman Empire itself was designed by rapacious criminals who looted and despoiled the provincials, and Robert Clive and Warren Hastings did much the same for Britain. While the man of letters Edmund Burke rhetorized in Parliament and helped lose the American colonies, Warren Hastings was working to build an empire. Moriarty describes these processes as examples of what he calls the 'dialectic' of history, of which he says Marx and Hegel are the supreme expositors.

"For the life of me, Watson, I cannot make out what the 'dialectic' means, but I fear that its incantation by Moriarty is a prelude to evil. The professor seems to mean what he writes. I had the feeling that he was really planning to put into practice his blueprint for a syndicate of crime. Do you realize how our lone-working inspectors of Scotland Yard—Lestrade, Hopkins, Mac-Donald—would find themselves out-organized, outmaneuvered, and outclassed by a criminal organization directed by Professor Moriarty? Our banks would cease to be impregnable strong-boxes; politicians would tremble lest their assassinations might be commissioned by their rivals; a network of illegal power, ramifying through the whole society, would inflict terror on whomsoever they chose. Would our British parliamentary system, based on fair play and toleration, survive the obliteration of virtue?"

"My dear Holmes," I responded, "surely you attach too much importance to a speculative philosophical disquisition written by an obscure mathematical coach. It can scarcely have any bearing on your securing the return of Eleanor Marx to the safe environs of her mother and father."

"You speak with good English common sense, Watson, and I am grateful to you for it. Often, however, I follow my detective's instinct. It is like that of a dog pursuing the scent of its quarry, or the scientist impelled by an intuition as to the law of nature underlying the disparate phenomena he is studying. I could never explain to you how that intuition works, but I have always felt that the

Reverend William Whewell was right in thinking that Mill's inductive methods were unworkable without its illuminating candle. I do apprehend that Professor Moriarty, the friend of Edward B. Aveling, may soon play his hand in our little affair. Especially did I feel this at luncheon today when Karl Pearson enlightened me as to the circumstances of Moriarty's resignation from the professorship of mathematics at Liverpool."

"Karl Pearson? I have heard his name mentioned, but I am finding it hard to distinguish among the many persons I have met this week and the various names I have heard, all of whom are active participants in this social ferment that I have been observing without imbibing."

"I met Karl Pearson through Mr. Shaw this noon. Our stalwart Irish bookworm espied me at my reading and promptly invited me once more to take my noon meal, with him and Karl Pearson, at his 'vegetarian vivarium,' as he put it. Pearson is a brilliant young mathematician in his mid-twenties; he was a Wrangler at Cambridge. Third, as I recall. He also spent a year in Germany, where he was converted to socialism, became an admirer of Marx, and had his room searched by the Prussian police for concealed Marxist literature. He changed the spelling of his given name from C-a-r-l to K-a-r-l—a bit of hero-worship, I imagine—wrote a novel about his German experiences, and then asked Karl Marx for permission to translate *Das Kapital* into English. He met the old revolutionist. Pearson doesn't like to talk about what happened. Evidently the old man didn't take to the sharp young mathematician. Marx feels most at home with his coterie of worshipful Internationalists, journalists, printers, and carpenters, but he fears meeting men abler in the sciences than himself. Marx said he didn't like Pearson's translation, though Pearson is a thorough scholar in German literature and history. Pearson knows both Aveling and Eleanor Marx; he thinks the first a fraud and the second a hysteric. But he knows all about Moriarty, whom he regards as a good mathematician with solid work to his credit but with no exceptional originality.

"Pearson thinks that's where the trouble began. Moriarty was a candidate for the professorship of mathematics at the University of Liverpool at which he was lecturing. At this juncture, a great mathematician, William Kingdon Clifford of London's University

College, died abroad. Somehow Moriarty got permission from Clifford's widow to examine her husband's unpublished mathematical papers; whereupon he extracted one on non-Euclidean geometry, a subject with which he had not previously been concerned. Moriarty submitted this paper as his own for publication to the London Mathematical Society; there it was discovered to be identical with one that Clifford had submitted two years earlier. The Society had been waiting for his return to correct the difficult proofs. To avoid a public exposure of his plagiarism and thievery, Moriarty resigned from his post at Liverpool. He and Aveling, both embittered against society, wallow in their bitterness. Their characters are similar alloys of ability, envy-propelled hatred, and the desire to exert power over men. 'Science,' says Pearson, 'was once the pursuit of isolated recluses who studied the laws of phenomena and verified them for sheer love of knowledge. Now it is becoming an avenue for talented men through which they can acquire power and prestige in society. Moriarty and Aveling are two extreme cases of this trend.' "

"I think you are concerning yourself unduly, my dear Holmes, with this mathematical coach, Robert Owen Moriarty, whose name must have gone to his head. Evidently as an Owenite he believes in communizing another man's work, especially if the man is dead. I often think, Holmes, that parents should be prohibited from naming children after illustrious historical personages. The children are obliged to wear mantles highly alien to their characters, and the effect must be deleterious. A name should not stand in the way of a personality realizing itself. Now your Christian name, Sherlock, is properly anonymous and noncommittal."

"I dare say it is, Watson, though Irene Adler dared ask whether it was perchance derived from Shylock."

We both laughed heartily. "But Holmes, I inquired, "you have not told me whether you encountered Eleanor Marx at the British Museum."

Holmes's face drew back for a moment as if with the recollection of an unpleasant scene. "Yes," he said, "I did meet Miss Marx at the library. She accompanied me to a small readers' establishment for tea and scones. She was still upset over the cruel way in which Edward Aveling had used Amy Levy, but she kept assuring me: 'Edward is really not like that at all. He's kind and loving and gentle. He is a poet, a Shelleyan, and he does believe in the exalting power of love. Every once in a while, however, his harsh upbringing asserts itself. His father, you know, is a Protestant minister whose life has been built on abstention, abnegation, and abjuration.' "

"I told her, Watson, that I would be frank with her, that Mr. Friedrich Engels had been to see me, that I had talked briefly with her father, Dr. Karl Marx, who was most distressed at her disappearance. I said that usually in such a case my sympathies were with the daughter who, having probably encountered some worthy young man whom she wished to marry, was being forbidden to do so by some harsh father or unkind mother. My responsibility usually ended when I informed the parents of their daughter's whereabouts and conveyed the news that she was well and happy with her excellent husband and deserved their consideration and affection.

" 'In your case, however, Miss Marx,' I said, 'if I may persist in addressing you thus, I feel a far deeper responsibility. Miss Marx, Edward Aveling is, in my opinion, a man of despicable character. He practices vices that I cannot bring myself to describe to you. Your own generous and self-sacrificing character can only become debased by sharing such a man's life, for you will be compelled to connive at his flouting the moral code of all humankind. He will finally treat you as he treats others—as instruments for his own misuse—indifferent that he pollutes their lives. He may well destroy you, or leave you helpless, alone, and friendless, after having extracted from you the use of your youth, your body, your name, your inheritance, your talents, your loyalties. He will then throw you aside, discard you like old clothing, to seek for himself something more à la mode. I beseech you, Miss Marx, to leave this man and to return to your family. If, for some reason, you cannot bring yourself to return to your mother and father, then I implore you, Miss Marx, to move for a while to the home of your friend Miss Irene Adler. She loves you much. You can then reflect calmly for as long as you wish on your recent experiences. You will be able to discuss them with a good friend and, in so doing, your own judgment will become clearer and your decision more grounded in your own best longings.'

"Eleanor Marx regarded me helplessly with her fawnlike eyes. She seemed wounded, inexpressibly so. She said she couldn't feel angry with me. All her life, her father had taught her to have contempt for all police spies; they had arrested his friends and spread horrible lies about himself, alleging either that Karl Marx was a secret conspirator or a paid agent of Bismarck. Her father had indeed to write a whole book refuting the slander that he was a blackmailer and a police spy. 'But you, Mr. Holmes, are an independent, petty bourgeois detective, attached to no police organization; my father consulted you in his desperation and I can well understand that. There are things however that have happened in the intimacy of our family that I cannot disclose. I have chosen to leave my father's household. I shall remain with Edward Aveling.'

"I literally pleaded with her, Watson, as I have never pleaded before. She was preparing her own worst misery, I said. Her father and mother, I surmised, were neither to live much longer. If they died in her absence, she would torment herself with remorse. If she returned, they would doubtless honor every wish of hers and respect her privacy. On the other hand, if they learned that she was living with Edward Aveling in an unmarried state, the shame and shock might kill them both. Karl Marx, whatever he may have written against bourgeois ways, has no respect for women who give themselves out of wedlock. He is filled with a sense of decorum and cherishes a romantic conception of womanhood. In his eyes, his own daughter would be forever sullied as a fallen woman; he could never again address her without feeling her tainted, stained. Engels would then doubtless plead with him to recognize his own Tussy and not to withdraw his love from her. But Karl Marx would as leave have his daughter turn terrorist as see her the common-law mistress of a married scoundrel. Was it too much to ask that for a year or so, Eleanor might consent to dwell with her family? Then calmly, with her father and mother probably gone and her resentments obsolete, she could choose her own way of life. Thus her acts would be conceived not in rebellion but in reflection. I asked her again to allow me to escort her home.

"Eleanor Marx was affected by what I said. She looked tearfully, distressfully, about her. For a moment she sobbed and said:

'This is, as James Thomson said, a city of dreadful night that we inhabit. We deceive ourselves with our illusions of love and decency
and progress. We are animals like the apes, except that to their
animal ways we add the human vices of dishonesty and hypocrisy.
Life will never be what we would dream, and we are at best proud
prisoners. Only death disenthralls.'

" 'You are young, highly gifted, with a knowledge far beyond
most men and women, Miss Marx,' I replied, 'and if I may also say
without presumption, you are attractive and witty. You have the
calling to help humankind and all the powers required to realize
that calling. Surely, Miss Marx, the bitter words of pessimism cannot be your final philosophy.'

" 'Mr. Holmes,' she said as we arose from our melancholy tea,
'I have already arranged to visit Irene Adler at her rooms tomorrow
evening. Might I ask you to join us after dinner?'

"I agreed most willingly. I am hopeful, my dear Watson, that
tomorrow evening Eleanor Marx will decide to return to her family.
Fortunately, she will be advised tomorrow by 'the Woman,' her
wisest friend, Miss Irene Adler. I never thought I would render
such a service to the Socialist International, and to the author of its
Bible, *Das Kapital*—Dr. Karl Marx.''

"Politics," I mumbled in reply, "makes strange bedfellows of
us all."

"No," said Holmes. "It's rather that the struggle for existence
underlying class struggles sometimes is tempered by the sense of
humanity, by what the Greeks called *agape*."

"Working among the socialists, and speaking the language of
comrades, seems to be turning you towards them, my dear
Holmes."

"There is small likelihood of that, Watson, though 'comrade' is
a beautiful word that Walt Whitman introduced into the language
of politics. I cannot help fearing, however, that the crimes that will
be done in its name will far outnumber those wrought in the name
of 'liberty.' ''

Chapter Six

Holmes meanwhile could evidently not put out of his mind the article by Professor Moriarty.

"Watson," he said, "I don't think you have sufficiently grasped the stupendous significance of Professor Moriarty's reflections on the future of crime in the twentieth century. That man has a deeper insight than anyone who has ever lived into the mainsprings of crime and the protean forms it will take as our society presumably progresses. He inverts the complacent prediction of progress into a disconcerting forecast of regress. He is the strategist of crime and, if he were equally its tactician, there's no telling to what realm of evil he might yet lead England. And he has the genius to pose an alliance between the new criminality and the new revolutionary movement to constitute a new oligarchy that could have the world do its bidding. He will see to it that any rival Workers' International will be reduced into little more than a hymn-singing society."

Suddenly Holmes proposed that we drop in on Marx's house. "The old man of Maitland Park Road will be pleased to see us. He keeps late hours and prefers late visitors. Besides, it's still early in the evening. We can tell him that we've seen and spoken with his daughter, that she's well, and that we hope she will soon be under his roof again. And we shall invoke the assistance of his vast erudition; he can tell us what Bakunin's project for humanity portends. Watson, there's more at stake here for the future of Britain, America, and Europe than in all our petty wars with Indian princelings and tribesmen.''

Twenty minutes later we were seated again with a welcoming Karl Marx before his slow-burning fireplace in his book-lined library; more than ever its walls seemed like fortified works constructed of books and pamphlets. I wondered whether this Great Wall of Literature made Marx impervious to reality. Marx watched me as I surveyed them and said mischievously, "Young revolutionists make their barricades out of paving stones; an old one such as I will make his barricade of books.''

Holmes then informed Marx briefly that he was communicating with his daughter Eleanor; knew her whereabouts, and hoped for her return in the near future. Marx, much pleased, obviously reposed much confidence in Holmes. He began reminiscing with the spontaneous associations of old age. He understood Tussy's problems well, he said, for he too had been young once. Those had been stormy years that had preceded the mighty revolt of 1848; he himself had been a source of grave concern, said Karl Marx, to his own father, who had watched him wasting his time at several universities, writing poems and plays, studying Hegel, the history of art, mythology, and philosophy, even getting arrested once for being tipsy; the hard-working lawyer had warned his son against spending his nights with a club of unemployed doctors of philosophy arguing whether Jesus existed or was a historical myth. His father, said Karl Marx, remained a diligent, bourgeois Jew to the end, even though he was obliged for professional reasons to declare himself a Christian, and the father would have preferred his son to master medicine or the law instead of embarking on the uncertain career of journalism. "And maybe my father wasn't altogether wrong,'' said Marx, "when he predicted that the devil in me—a 'dybbuk,' he called it—would bring sorrow and tears into the life of my betrothed Jenny von Westphalen. The old Jew was a Kantian who took the sense of duty seriously, whereas I felt myself an integral part of the World-Historical Spirit.''

Holmes gently interposed that an article he had just read on crime much interested him; its author was a follower of one Michael Bakunin. Marx's head reared at the mention of Bakunin's name; indeed, his beard seemed to bristle with readiness for battle.

"It is well that the disciple takes Bakunin as an authority on crime, for that Russian all his life worked for an alliance between communism, amorality, and violence. True, he was a forty-eighter and behaved well in the Dresden fighting, but he was a sick, half-crazy man who made a principle out of having no principles and proclaimed as his revolutionist's creed that to destroy the existing society he would adopt whatever means were necessary to achieve the end."

"But wasn't Bakunin a loyal revolutionist who languished in Russian dungeons and Siberian solitude for the sake of the movement?" queried Holmes. "Didn't he join the International?"

The fire in Marx had re-awakened. "I do not deny that Bakunin made sacrifices for the revolutionary cause, Mr. Holmes. His courage deserted him, however, in prison. Through our most trusted Russian sources we know that Bakunin wrote a most abject Confession and Appeal to the Czar himself while he was in jail. After a while, they allowed him to go to Siberia as an exile, where they conveniently helped him to escape by ship to America. Do you know, Mr. Holmes, I have observed that those who dwell in the fantasy of subterranean secret societies have a grandiosity that is the antithesis to their impotence. Your friend Dr. Watson is a physician, and he will know what I mean. All Bakunin's secret comrades knew about it. Bakunin was a man only in a formal sense; he was not a man in the dialectical relation with women, and the child that was born to his wife was not his. And this man, deluded with make-believe, allowed himself to be dragged into an intrigue that came near disgracing the international working-class movement. He became infatuated with a Russian youth; the two organized themselves, all two of them, into the 'World Revolutionary Alliance.' The youth, Nechayev by name, went back to Russia, where after betraying several revolutionary students to the Czarist police he murdered another in the most brutal fashion to demonstrate his claim to pseudomanhood. Then he escaped to Switzerland, where he tried to seduce as well as extort money from the young sister of a famous friend of Bakunin's. Slowly Bakunin came to his senses, and realized that his 'boy' had made a fool of him.

"This is the man who would pretend to ignite the Russian Revolution, to make a new Peasants' Revolt. He claims that the

94

uncivilized Russian peasants and the backward races will make the socialist revolution. He says that the western European working-class are overcivilized, degenerate, effete; that their revolutionary instincts have been dissipated by civilization. He regards civilization as a sort of disease. You can't trust a Russian, Mr. Holmes. They have the cunning, cruelty, and duplicity of savages. You know the old proverb, Mr. Holmes, 'Scratch a Russian and you'll find a Tartar.' Those Russians are an unceasing threat to the winning of freedom in Western Europe. Their Cossack regiments executed the Hungarian democrats in Budapest in 1849, and they would relish doing the same with the German social democrats. Bakunin feels most at home with brigands, criminals, and terrorists. And if a European criminal party were to arise, officered by *déclassés,* attorneys without clients, teachers without pupils, doctors without patients, perpetual students with no professional aim, journalists with no newspaper, and with infantry ranks recruited from the lumpen-proletariat—scavengers, petty thieves, and cutthroats who have no desire to work in any society—Bakunin would regard them as the allies for his savage scythe-wielding *moujiks.* The criminal mind of the twentieth century will find in Bakunin its ideologist.''

"Surely, however, Dr. Marx, Bakunin nonetheless did aim to help establish a communist economy and, if I have understood your own views, you have asserted that the material existence of society, its economy, determines its law, politics, culture, and morals. Should you not therefore welcome the advent of communist society even if it is inaugurated under the auspices of Russian peasants and terrorist conspirators?''

Marx waved his left arm impatiently as he adjusted his pince-nez magisterially; he looked altogether the professor patiently trying to tutor a backward student through his elementary lessons.

"My dear Mr. Holmes," said Marx, "when I was young, and Engels and I were first formulating our materialistic conception of history, I allowed myself to make broad, sweeping statements. They were the idiom natural to the excited glow of first discovery and first insight, almost like first love. A young lover who tells his beloved in poems how beautiful she is doesn't append a series of provisos and qualifications. Those properly come later. And we had perceived a great truth that we wanted to enunciate clearly and emphatically. Moreover, we were polemicizing against the whole established school of metaphysical historians who had chosen to forget that before men can think, write philosophy, and engage in politics they must secure food, shelter, clothing; in short, make a living.

"Now, however, the society we live in is a civilized one, and that adjectival qualification counts. If Bakuninists were to make a communist revolution in backward Russia, their communism would resemble that of a primitive tribe. Their communism would be hostile to science, culture, art, and technology, to all that through the achievement of the highest intellect has elevated mankind. Their communism would be what we've called 'barracks communism,' where the freedom of the individual will be obliterated and one will be continuously supervised by police agents and industrial functionaries as one eats, works, plays, sleeps. Imagine a Sophocles trying to write an *Oedipus Rex* in a barracks communist regime that would forbid any drama on incest, or Shakespeare trying to write Hamlet's soliloquy on death in a way that would appease a Barracks Board of Censors. No, thank you. Such communism would be the enslavement of the proletariat, not their enfranchisement, Mr. Holmes!"

Marx had allowed himself to be carried away into an eloquence of speech. I wondered if he found his reply to Sherlock Holmes sufficiently convincing. For a moment, I speculated as a physician as to what the inner despair of a man might be who, in his old age, had come to doubt the truth of the ideas upon which he had boldly staked his life's work. Karl Marx had written books and articles in praise of socialism, but he seemed no more capable than any tyro in propaganda of replying to the most elementary objection to socialist schemes. Holmes fastened simply on the weakness of Marx's intellectual structure.

"Dr. Marx, I have read John Stuart Mill's essays and writings on socialism. Not only does he fear that a centrally administered economy will lack all those experimental centers of creativity that flourish in a planless society, but he foresees that it will also become inefficient; the incentive of a higher profit as a reward for originality in production will be much reduced in a socialist setting. The rule of mediocrities is common to all bureaucracies; a society completely controlled by bureaucrats would enthrone the hegemony of the third rate. Has any socialist answered Mill?'' asked Holmes.

"We have no need to answer John Stuart Mill," cried Karl Marx. "History will answer him for us. The mission of the working class is to achieve power; then its abilities and powers will prove themselves adequate to solving all the questions as to how to administer the socialist society. We do not draw up blueprints or charts for future socialist bureaucrats; we expect the workers to get along without them, and we leave the making of maps for the future to Utopian romancers. When history will pose its problems to the working class, it will at the same time give them the tools for solving them."

"That is a noble faith, Dr. Marx," said Holmes, "but if I mistake not the lesson taught by Darwin and Winwood Reade, the past's record silently testifies contrarily with its remains of extinct species who pursued evolutionary lines that foundered on insoluble problems. That's why Reade could call his great book *The Martyrdom of Man*."

Marx reflected for some moments, as if summoning up new reserves of confidence. "Mr. Holmes," he said, "I am second to no one in my admiration for Charles Darwin. His book, overflowing with facts, overthrew, as no philosopher could have done, the last excuse for any belief in God. But the blind, anarchic struggle for existence comes to an end with the rise of the human species. Humankind is endowed with reason, and reason makes possible foresight and invention; it brings salvation to replace martyrdom. It is the highest stage of the world-historical evolution. The kingdom of liberation supersedes the vale of martyrdom; instead of hymns to perpetual sorrow, humanity will sing endless refrains to a dialectical transfiguration."

We took our leave from Karl Marx, and we asked him to convey

HOLMES WAS SILENT AS WE RETURNED IN A HANSOM CAB TO
BAKER STREET.

our respects to the ailing Mrs. Marx. Holmes was silent as we
returned in a hansom cab to Baker Street. As he sat down in
another new Morris chair that Mrs. Hudson had provided, he
remarked, "Marx has the satisfaction of a philosopher's vision, but
those who try to realize it, like his daughter Eleanor, will forfeit with
frustrated lives, especially as it transpires that Marx's vision was the
facile imagery of a fantasist rather than a scientific prevision."

Then, as if imbibing optimism from his Morris chair, Holmes
remarked, "However, grandiose social movements, let us not
forget, have happier tangential consequences. William Morris
preaches a return to medieval crafts and guilds; the world is pleased
to accept his comfortable chairs and cheerful wallpaper. Robert

Owen preached socialist factories; the world accepts his notion of schools for adults. Shaw's comedies may make people laugh long after they have forgotten his socialist crotchets.''

Chapter Seven

he next morning I left early to attend at the hospital's Section for Tropical Diseases. A ship was recently arrived from the Pacific Island of New Caledonia, and several of its seamen were afflicted with a strange fever. I had been summoned to be part of a consulting physicians group. Very soon after examining the dejected sailors, who seemed to be expecting an affliction at least as dramatic as leprosy, I was able to join in reassuring them that theirs was a well-known variety of dengue fever and that a few days of rest and quiet living would expel its symptoms.

The sailors began talking cheerfully of their experiences. They had stopped at Marseilles to disembark a whole cargo of "Communard" exiles returning from New Caledonia to France. I had been quite unaware that after the brief civil war in France in 1871, several thousands of Paris Communards had been deported from France to New Caledonia. They included anarchists and terrorists, but also Marxist Internationalists. The sailors were much impressed when I told them that I had had the pleasure of a brief meeting with Dr. Karl Marx. They then looked upon me as if I had seen Moses himself descending from Mt. Sinai and bearing the tablets of the Law. They spoke most reverently about a woman anarchist, Louise Michel, the "Red Virgin" they called her, who throughout all her years of island exile had remained faithful to her anarchist creed. She had ministered to the sick, brought good cheer to all, and founded a school. Even the Kanaka cannibal tribesmen revered her. They told me a bitter, savage war of extinction had broken out two or three years previously between the French colonists and the Kanakas. It began because the white settlers were seizing Kanaka women. The cannibal natives killed and consumed several villages of French colonists. They attacked Thio, where Louise Michel had gone on an errand of mercy to the convict laborers in the nickel mines. They killed and dined on the mining managers but spared Louise. Amongst themselves, however, the Communards quarreled fiercely; more than half were hostile to the cannibal uprising, though some were sympathetic.

I remarked to them that they should tell Dr. Marx of these last experiences of the Paris Communards. Evidently, the ties of blood and race had proved themselves stronger than those of one's occupation, possessions, or politics. The sailors agreed but insisted communism was a beautiful ideal. I felt however that an ideal that was contrary to the realities of human nature would finally lead people to pitfalls and mishaps; a social policy could not be wise, it seemed to me, unless it were founded on a true social anatomy and social physiology. "But you are a *bourgeois,*" the sailors told me good-naturedly.

These thoughts were in my mind as I returned to our Baker Street rooms in the late afternoon. I found Sherlock Holmes sitting moodily in his chair, with his hands raised and joined at the fingertips in an acute angle. I thought to cheer him by telling him of my strange encounter with the crew of seamen returned from New Caledonia and their stories of the Paris Communards.

"Think of it," I cried, "the fame of Dr. Karl Marx, a German-Jewish erudite living in London, reaches across oceans to the isolated cannibal island of New Caledonia."

"I wish, my dear Watson, that I could be sanguine about that influence. But I spent my luncheon hour this afternoon in the laboratory at the University College with the brilliant young zoologist Professor Edwin Ray Lankester. I am surprised, indeed, that he is the good friend and wise counselor of the aging Dr. Karl Marx. And with Lankester was another brilliant young man, Charles Waldstein, a lecturer in the history of ancient Greek art at King's College. He too is a good friend of Dr. Marx. I have not ever been with two more brilliant young men in my life. In fact, this case of the revolutionist's daughter has transformed me into a kind of pilgrim listening to the Canterbury Tales of his fellow travelers. How have you and I, my dear Watson, contrived to remain so utterly insulated from these novel ideas that are exciting so many of our contemporaries?

"I had written last week to Edwin Ray Lankester, after Engels told me he was a friend of Marx's. I requested the pleasure of a meeting with him on a confidential question that concerned the welfare of Karl Marx. I ventured to presume that my own work would be known to one who had played the most active part in the exposure of the fraudulent medium, Henry Slade. Professor Lankester responded most cordially with an invitation to luncheon, informing me as well that he would endeavor to have his friend and colleague Charles Waldstein join us. Thus I have enjoyed this noon eggs that were boiled over a Bunsen burner, breads that were heated in an incubation chamber, and salt that issued from a test tube labeled 'NaCl.' Two more charming and cultivated companions I have not met.

"Lankester is a well-sized young man with a strong square head and an already ample and imposing abdomen. He wears his gown even at lunch, perhaps an old Oxford habit. His voice booms out his opinions as if they were broadsides fired at the enemy. He got to know Marx through Waldstein, who, in turn, was introduced to Marx by a Russian scholar. Marx plied Lankester with questions about the world of English science. He wanted to know all about Charles Darwin and Thomas Henry Huxley, what manner of men they were, what they read, how they comported themselves, what their families were like. Lankester has known both Darwin and Huxley since he was a boy. He answered all of Marx's questions with direct personal detail. Marx commented sadly that, while he as a youth at Bonn and Berlin was fighting verbal battles over ideology and theology, Darwin and Huxley and Wallace spent their formative years exploring strange seas and jungles and mountains and savage peoples to learn of nature, to collect specimens, to add to man's knowledge of the world.

" 'They discovered new species and novel truth, while I polemicized with pamphleteers,' said Marx sadly.

"Lankester was dismayed by the depression into which Marx

had fallen. Partially, no doubt the illness that was whittling away his wife's strength was laying Marx's spirits low. But Marx too was one who took little exercise, led an irregular life, smoked cigars incessantly, and suffered continually from carbuncles. Lankester indeed felt that when Marx joked about taking his carbuncles out on the capitalist system, he wasn't altogether joking. To elevate Marx's spirits, Lankester reminded Marx that workingmen in many lands regarded him as leader and spokesman, that the legislation being enacted in Britain and France to alleviate the lot of the working class was in no small measure the abiding outcome of Marx's work. Marx said he envied Darwin's walking with Professor John Henslow to discuss truths of natural science; how much healthier an intellectual provender that was than Bruno Bauer's discussions of the Gospels; how much more satisfying to regard at the end of one's life one's set of scientific papers rather than one's collection of inflammatory editorials. Above all, Marx is much interested in a little book by Lankester that was recently published entitled *Degeneration*. The young zoologist emphasizes the truth that many more species have retrogressed than have progressed, that there is no law of progress, as Spencer and indeed Karl Marx himself have believed. The Roman retrogression that led civilization backward to a loss of culture, science, learning, and industry in western Europe could have its analogue in modern times. Our society might become more simplified, losing those organs grown obsolete with diminished functions even as barnacles and shrimps regressed from their ancestral species.

"Lankester remarked that *Degeneration* seemed to fit Marx's present mood. 'Thirty years ago Marx would have composed a vitriolic, multi-epitheted brochure lampooning me for depicting nature with the biased line of one who, as an academician of a declining bourgeois class, magnified the transient defeat of that class into a world-scientific principle.'

"As for Eleanor Marx, said Lankester, Waldstein knew her much better. She is the only daughter of Marx's still unmarried and living at home. She is her father's daughter and regards the mother as rather backward intellectually. She worships her father, and can not endure any criticism of him. But that sort of hero-worship entails its penalties. She has periods of intense depression, during which she refuses food. She imitates her father by keeping late hours, working feverishly on her translations or essays. She refuses to argue with people who have serious intellectual disagreements with her father; they simply haven't studied the subject sufficiently, she says. She goes to the meetings of the gas workers and devotedly does the secretarial chores for their union, preparing cards, membership lists, notices; it is all unpaid work and done with a religious fervor. At a union meeting, she thinks she is experiencing the most vivid enactment of the abstract pages of her father's book; the expropriated are gradually bestirring themselves to expropriate the expropriators. Lankester is convinced she will waste her life and talents, that she will write nothing that will have more than a journalistic significance, and that, when Marx dies, she probably will throw herself away on some scamp. She has been seen with one such at the University College, Edward Aveling, whom Lankester knows well, having been on the committee that read his doctoral thesis. Aveling took his degree to establish his superiority in Bohemian circles, but he lacks the self-mastery required for patient scientific research. He talks much not about the life of a scientist but of a scientific way of life, which in turn he makes equivalent to an unbridled exploitation and extortion practiced upon others. Lankester fears that Aveling may bring much discredit upon the name of science and has carefully refrained from recommending him for any of the professorships in provincial universities.

"I dare say Edwin Ray Lankester told me little that I did not already know or had inferred. His friend Charles Waldstein brought, however, some surprises. This young scholar of Greek art spoke with the most curious combination of accents: a pronunciation largely New Yorkish, I gather, together with some Germanism superimposed on his vowels and the overtones of Oxonian intonations attached to his sentences. He said Marx was fond of nothing more than to spend, for instance, long hours talking with him about the Parthenon frieze and the aesthetic theories of German philosophers. Marx comes to life when he talks of these youthful interests of his, but loses zest when political issues arise. Waldstein thought Marx was a literary man who fell in with the wrong circle in the 1840s and has been forever since entrapped in the role of economist and politician, which he inwardly detests. Waldstein says Marx really knows little about the working class. He has always kept away from their meetings and, when he has had to speak, lapsed into a florid and didactic type of speech that British workers found offensive. Waldstein says that Marx bitterly regrets that his two other daughters married socialists, and Frenchmen at that. He wishes they had wed Englishmen with stable characters devoted to their professions and indifferent to ideology.

"According to Waldstein, Marx said, 'That my daughter Laura chose to marry a West Indian nigger doctor who prefers politics to patients is Jehovah's revenge on me.'

" 'When he met me and discovered that I was a Jew, he seemed unusually pleased,' said Waldstein. 'Then I noticed that he tried to have Eleanor Marx be with me as much as he could manage; he would then relax and laugh approvingly at my witticisms. He began to address me by the German familiar pronoun *du,* asking me to do so as well. He even presented me with a photograph of himself, with a most generously flattering inscription. He minded not at all that I persistently reiterated that I did not accept the materialistic conception of history, that I felt it was an inadequate basis for interpreting the history of art and that, moreover, I gravely doubted whether the working class was the supreme progressive agency in history. Finally, I said flatly that I had no desire to live in a socialist society in which I was certain those activities that I cherished most, the arts, literature, and the sciences, would be stifled under the control of petty-minded party despots and party committees. Marx seemed pleased that my father was a prosperous merchant in New York; once he said that he would have liked to visit America, perhaps even to have lived there. He approved that I was lecturing at King's College and Cambridge, and he spent long hours with me in the collections of Greek art. He watched benignly when Mrs. Marx formally invited me to bring my mother to their house for dinner and liked it when the two women became close friends. Slowly, from remarks that my mother allowed herself, I gathered that nothing would give Dr. and Mrs. Marx more pleasure than to know that their daughter Eleanor would become my wife. I was both flattered and embarrassed. I admired Marx greatly as a world figure, as a man of great culture and original ideas. I did not wish, to be sure, to become known as the son-in-law of the great Socialist

Internationalist; on the other hand, that reason would have weighed little with me if I had been in love with Eleanor Marx, which I was not; nor was she with me.'

"Eleanor, Waldstein feels, has had her head so filled since infancy with communist slogans that, when it comes to her personal life, she is like a ship without ballast on stormy seas. Her father has inveighed so much against the mythology of bourgeois ethics—explicating that the diverse moral codes reflect different class systems and that there is no universal moral law—that Eleanor Marx has no philosophy to live by. She has a keen moral sense of right and wrong but she feels her father has shown that it's a vestige of bourgeois inculcation. Thus she is left morally confused among the Bohemian set, at the mercy of libertines and freebooters such as Shaw and Aveling. All that she clings to at the last is the Moses-like model of her father's life. If, for any reason, he were to be found wanting, if her worship of him would collapse or even become clouded, she would be like an idolator whose idol has disintegrated. She would be desperate for its replacement, or die if her life's emptiness could no longer be filled.

"My dear Watson, I almost feel that I have reflected on the character of Eleanor Marx in the way that a dramatist studies his heroine. Her maladies and misfortunes seem to me, alas, to be those that will become more frequent in our society in the century to come; our industries will become more powerful, our sciences more comprehensive, but the human spirit that will bear these achievements will be corroded from within by the reagent of a conviction of meaninglessness. I have always numbered myself among those who bear the standard of science; I have cheered and always will cheer for Darwin, Huxley, Mill, and Spencer. But my cheers grow less loud and less confident as I meditate on the problems of the child of the scientific century, Eleanor Marx."

Holmes and I ate our dinner of mutton and potatoes quietly. The bustling entrance of Mrs. Hudson with her dishes punctuated the paragraphs of our silence, comforting us with her excellent Yorkshire-style cooking. Holmes commented that, having been spoiled by Mrs. Hudson's simple, naturally flavored dishes, he had little tolerance for either the precosities of French cooking, the soggy heaviness of the German, or the garlicky encirclement of the

Russian. Neither of us looked forward to our next meeting with Eleanor Marx. The bitter tears of a young woman, her possibly unavailing struggle with evolving personal tragedy, left us dispirited and worried. There was little of the joy of the chase and capture that had often filled the last hours of Holmes's other cases. Nor could we advise our clients, or Eleanor Marx herself, to consult the guidance of their religious ministers; these were atheists all, the advocates of irreligion, and Sherlock Holmes perforce became in their secularist travail the representative of wisdom.

Chapter Eight

e proceeded after dinner to the flat of Miss Irene Adler. She greeted us both warmly at the door; Holmes's eyes were alight with a pleasure that they rarely showed; her warmth seemed to dissipate his deep dejection as the sunshine scatters the clouds. Eleanor Marx then approached us with a sad smile, yet welcoming us as friends.

Miss Adler began: "Eleanor and I have had a long talk. There is much that we discussed that we would not repeat to our male friends, even those whom we admire and trust. But I shall not say more. Eleanor will tell you what she has decided."

Eleanor Marx looked firmly at us, though her voice trembled slightly: "I have thought over carefully all that you have conveyed to me, Mr. Holmes, and I have considered as honestly as I can what my own responsibilities as well as my rights are. I do not agree with my friend Mr. Bernard Shaw in thinking that the quintessence of Ibsenism is to repudiate the notion of duty, that 'stern daughter of the voice of God,' in Wordsworth's phrase, as outmoded and bourgeois; I am not a self-worshiper. What torments my own father may have experienced or be experiencing, what agonies my mother may have undergone and muted in her long-suffering life, I do not know. I can conjecture, however, that their wounds have brought great pain and that they wish to see my life hopefully safe-guarded from the humiliations they have known, to see my marriage, if it takes place, not as one that condemns me to a life beset with gossip, insecurity, insults, poverty. My father remembers the years in which we children went hungry and became adept at eluding the bill-bearers at our door. I have my own duties, nonetheless, to my self, the right to fashion my own life, to realize what I regard as its goods.

"I shall return therefore to my father's house only under certain conditions: Neither he nor my mother is to interfere with my choice of friends or way of life; I shall be permitted to go from the house and return to it at whatever hours I choose, and no objection shall be made to those with whom I choose to spend my time. They may expect, of course, that I shall always observe the precepts of decency and decorum. Second, they shall allow me to become as financially independent as I can, through my own earnings in writing, translating, teaching, acting. And, third, even if my social hours would be spent with a man who is in a legal sense not eligible to be my husband, my father and mother shall make no objection. I would, however, not insist on bringing the man into my father's house. Under those conditions, Mr. Holmes, I shall be ready to return to Maitland Park Road, not as a prodigal daughter but as an independent, self-respecting grown woman. If my father and mother consent to these conditions, I shall be waiting tomorrow evening at my household with Irene, and forthwith will return to live with my father and mother. Irene will escort me and help with my belongings. And now I shall leave, and alone, if you permit me. I can perfectly well take care of myself and find my way back to the 'Jews' Den.' I want to tell Edward all I have decided."

Slowly she placed her cloak around her shoulders. She and Irene Adler embraced and kissed each other. Holmes insisted, however, on seeing her to the street and into a hansom cab.

As Miss Adler and I waited for him to return, she asked me with her unquenchable vivacity: "Pray, tell me, Dr. Watson, how do you find Mr. Holmes as a companion with whom to live?"

For a moment I was at loss for words because I had never had such a prying question put to me; furthermore, there was an impish tone to her query. Regaining my composure, I said: "Miss Adler, I have always found Mr. Sherlock Holmes a most considerate partner in our joint lodgings. He respects his companion's moods and privacy. When I wish to meditate, read, or simply watch the fire idly, he does not intrude. I must amend that, however. Every once in a while he will join my meditation, having by some striking series of deductions fathomed exactly the character of the reflection that occupied me. He does smoke his pipe frequently, which leads to some annoyance for our landlady, Mrs. Hudson. On the other hand, he has a connoisseur's taste in tobacco. His chemical experiments are sometimes a nuisance, especially when our living room becomes a maze of flowing pipettes and sizzling retorts; there is the recompense, however, of his beautifully lucid explanations

OUR LIVING ROOM BECOMES A MAZE OF FLOWING PIPETTES AND
SIZZLING RETORTS.

of chemical theories, so that I have found living with him the equivalent of residence at a university. Then the evening comes with his violin singing into the empyrean. You must hear Holmes's renditions of Mendelssohn's *Songs Without Words;* their blend of classical with romantic seems most congruent with Holmes's character. And living with Holmes is also like taking a degree in what Herbert Spencer calls 'sociology.' I have been reading much in the newspapers lately of the social surveys that are being undertaken by Charles Booth and his coworkers studying the life and labor of the people of London. Well, I can assure you, Miss Adler, that Mr. Sherlock Holmes is the ablest sociologist in England. To his sitting-room come men and women of all classes, from prime minister to homeless seaman, from the wealthy and well endowed to the struggling and impoverished, from university students and dons to the illiterate and sordid.''

Miss Irene Adler listened most interestedly, then without shyness, said: "I should very much like visiting your rooms, Dr. Watson, and observing from within the house at Baker Street that I once saw from a hansom cab as I teased and outwitted Mr. Holmes, then the consultant to a pompous relic of a declining European order.''

"We found that prince, Miss Adler, a most amiable person who still professed the utmost admiration for your person.''

"I think Mr. Holmes's talents are wasted upon such people.''

"Had it not been, however, for that case of, shall I call it, a scandal in Bohemia, Mr. Holmes would not have had the rare good fortune to meet you, Miss Adler.''

Miss Irene Adler's dark eyes illumined her face with merriment. Even at this hour, when our hearts were heavy with the tragic bewilderment of her friend Eleanor Marx, Miss Adler refused to dwell on the sadness of things; she preferred to laugh with the gods. If she was a materialist philosopher, she was one like the laughing Greek sage Democritus. She and Eleanor Marx were utterly unlike in character. Eleanor Marx had the literary knowledge, the idealistic aspiration, and the easy competence that comes with growing up in a scholar's workshop; but Eleanor had inherited also from her father his personal incompetence in resolving life's problems. Her spirit seemed inhabited by a will to make her own existence as difficult as possible. Irene Adler, on the contrary, touched all things with grace; she held to socialist ideals not out of a sense of duty but rather because she felt that such a life would be so much more interesting and joyous. Eleanor was a disciple of the suffering prophet Isaiah; Irene Adler preferred the understanding sage Ecclesiastes.

Shortly, Holmes returned. "Watson," he said, "We have no time to lose. We must be off to tell old Engels that Miss Marx might be ready to return to her family's dwelling tomorrow."

He shook hands warmly with Irene Adler. "Miss Adler," he said, "if the case of Eleanor Marx has a happy denouement, I hope you will accept the invitation to be the dinner guest of Dr. Watson and myself at the new American restaurant, Luckow's."

"It would be a pleasure for me, Mr. Holmes, though I should prefer to be your guest at one of Mrs. Hudson's dinners at 221B Baker Street."

Holmes was startled. She continued: "After all, Mr. Holmes, that was the headquarters where you conceived the strategic plan to penetrate my household, and it would be fitting that I now occupy yours."

Holmes laughed, and said: "It shall be as you please, Miss Adler, though Mrs. Hudson will be most surprised."

Soon we were at Engels's house at Regent's Park Road not far from the Marx establishment. Fortunately, Engels never went to bed before midnight and he was most convivial at ten o'clock when we arrived. He listened to Holmes's narrative, and most closely to the conditions stipulated by Eleanor Marx as the basis for her resuming life with her parents.

Engels said: "Marx and I agree on almost all political and economic questions, but in late years we do not see eye to eye on questions of personal morality. It was otherwise when we were young, when he and I both believed in untrammeled love, like our great guide Feuerbach. We even wrote some passionate lines on the can-can dance and tropical passion in a book that nobody has read in thirty-five years. I have continued in my unmarried state all my life, except for a few days when I consented to marry my dying Irish companion, Mary Burns; it comforted her Catholic soul. But, on the whole, I have continued to believe in free love. Marx, on the other hand, would hear none of it as his three daughters grew to maidenhood. No father has ever stood more faithful vigil over the virtue of his daughters. He almost sent one future son-in-law packing when he wooed daughter Laura with an overwarm tropical zeal.

I don't know much about this Aveling, but at least he's a doctor of science and not a Proudhonist or a Blanquist like the others. And if Eleanor likes him, I'd not be disposed to argue. In any case, I shall urge the Moor to accept Eleanor's conditions. Let us go to Marx's place directly. He will still be up for at least another hour."

"I shall not argue with you, Mr. Engels, concerning the personal character of Dr. Edward Aveling. The hour is too late for me to tell you my findings. But I can think of no choice for a lifelong intimacy who could be more disastrous for the personality and well-being of Miss Marx."

"Oh, tush, Mr. Holmes, you speak like a Kantian. I even detect a touch of the parsonage. But let us march over to Marx's."

A few minutes later we found Dr. Karl Marx sitting beside his table under a gaslight. Clothed in a dark-blue smoking jacket, his beard looking very gray and shaggy, his face, very tired, retained none of the fire one commonly associates with the revolutionist. A detached spectator, observing people's movements much as a natural philosopher records the directions and speeds of molecules, seemed to have replaced the revolutionary man of deeds. On the table was the little book *Degeneration* by Edwin Ray Lankester.

"I am writing to a Russian friend of mine about Lankester's book," said Marx. "A book with an unhappy message; so I hope you bring good tidings to me about my poor, unhappy child."

Very quickly Mr. Frederick Engels told Dr. Marx of Eleanor's readiness to return to the family home provided that her conditions were accepted. He told Marx that Eleanor had been living with a secularist scientist, Dr. Edward Aveling by name.

Marx blanched perceptibly at that and spoke nothing for a few moments. Then he said quietly: "I'd agree to anything to get Eleanor home again; I'd even retract the *Communist Manifesto*. After all, no individual is necessary to the socialist movement, but one person can be necessary to another. And I am a person, not a movement, and in my old age my family and children mean more to me than the whole unpleasant mass of warring, contending men. My wife is asleep in her room; any day she will die. I shall tell her as little as possible about all this."

We rose. Dr. Marx approached Sherlock Holmes, took his hand, and shook it warmly. "Mr. Holmes, I owe much to you. You have dealt with my daughter and myself with courtesy, consideration, and kindness. My own strength is failing and much that has happened makes me wonder from time to time where the truth in things lies. In my youth, I dedicated my life to the service of suffering humanity; I wished to see it ennobled. My studies, writings, and activities were all to this aim; I even sacrificed the health and lives of my dearest ones. Now my daughter's unhappiness rebukes me. Have I deluded myself? I do not know. I can only say, with Kant, that my motive was the highest—my will was good, yet my goodness may have been compounded with folly.''

Sherlock Holmes bowed deeply before the aged scholar-revolutionist, and he and I withdrew, leaving the two comrades of 1848 to themselves.

Chapter Nine

oon we were seated before the fire at Baker Street ruminating upon the evening's melancholy events. "The calling of a revolutionist," said Holmes, "is an utterly abnormal one. From what Lankester told us, Karl Marx was a rebellious, Byronic young student (there were many such in Europe) who cast his life on the lines of a play like *Manfred*—stormy, brooding, threatening, sacrificing, but deliberately choosing a life that had to be enveloped in personal tragedy, or at best in wasted years. We English don't have this phenomenon. I felt some rebellion against my professor of chemistry, but it was because he refused to accept Mendeleev's Periodic Principle and ridiculed it as Pythagorean moonshine. With great glee I read to him one day that Mendeleev's prediction of a missing element, eka-silicon, had indeed been verified. I was much too interested in my studies in natural science, which filled almost all my time, to take *Manfred* very seriously."

"My experience was much like yours, Holmes," I replied. "Our problems with our sick patients at Bart's were all the reality we could handle; they crowded out any need to conjure forth imaginary ones. The medical curriculum provided no place for anyone ambitious for either political power or the leadership of a revolutionary sect. Dr. Karl Marx, my dear Holmes, strikes me as a pathetic chap, a sorry figure in domestic misery who must still play the actor in world history, whose prophet he fancies himself. But then, Holmes, I found Isaiah and his fellow prophets so tedious and repugnant to me that I could never read them through in my Sunday School days. I refuse to believe that the British working class will ever attach itself to this man's theories. It is only where people go mad, as in Russia among the young nihilists, that they may look to Marx, precisely for his intellectual madness.''

''Perhaps you are right, my dear Watson. But the world is not made up of men of English common sense, such as yourself, who stand guard against history's waves of irrationality. I hope nothing goes amiss tomorrow, but I am not confident. We have heard nothing from Edward B. Aveling. I cannot believe he will let things lie. Perhaps he has been consulting with his colleague Moriarty, even while we were with Eleanor Marx and Miss Adler. We shall see.''

We joined each other at luncheon the next day; I had spent the morning at the Section for Tropical Diseases listening to a discussion of the new bacteriological theories concerning the causation of malaria, and welcomed with pleasure the herring, Yorkshire pudding, and boiling tea that the ever solicitous Mrs. Hudson set before Holmes and myself. Holmes was still examining an assortment of socialist books and journals that he said he had picked up at an obscure bookshop in Whitechapel: books by such authors as H. M. Hyndman, E. Belfort Bax, and William Morris; magazines like *Today* and the *Labor Standard* with articles by Engels; but also several pamphlet reprints of essays by Herbert Spencer against socialism, the coming slavery.

''A curious literature is this socialist outpouring, filled with moral indignation and righteous stance, but utterly devoid of any consideration as to the possible defects of the society they propose to establish,'' commented Holmes. ''They don't even try to refute Spencer, who says the socialist order will inaugurate a military-bureaucratic despotism; they simply ignore him. They say that the French revolutionists had no idea what kind of society they were trying to found, which isn't true at all, since the French middle-classes had gradually during many years been assuming the roles of administration and government. My grandmother Vernet used to tell us how her great-grandfather Pierre was a high judge in Bordeaux, and descended from the sage Montaigne, who was the city's mayor. If Herbert Spencer is right, and a socialist society

HOLMES WAS EXAMINING AN ASSORTMENT OF SOCIALISTS BOOKS
AND JOURNALS.

would inevitably become despotic, then it would be foolhardy to
rely on socialists who refuse to meet that fact. Once the despotism
exists, there will be no chance to raise the question. Marx and
Engels say it's Utopian to ask for a bill of particulars as to the
character of the socialist society. It seems to me more Utopian to
call for a faith that its character will assure the highest development
of man.''

"I entirely agree with you, Holmes," I replied. "I once read an
article by John Stuart Mill that said that behind the facade of every
revolutionary social scheme lurked the will of a liberticide. I think
that Bernard Shaw and his artistic friends never really ask
themselves how they would fare in a socialist society. Compelled to
gather clandestinely in hidden nooks, they would remember their

happy bourgeois Bohemian days before the socialist dictators enforced the end of all Bohemianism.''

There was a knock at the door, and Mrs. Hudson entered, bringing to our surprise a distraught-looking Eleanor Marx. "The young lady asked to be brought to you directly, Mr. Holmes," said Mrs. Hudson.

"Rest assured, Mrs. Hudson, that you acted wisely," said Holmes as she departed.

Eleanor Marx sank into our easy chair and began to sob. Holmes kindly patted her shoulder and comforted her. "Come, Miss Marx, you are among friends. We shall try to help in every way we can.''

"He will not let me go," said Miss Marx. "I have not slept all night. Edward Aveling berates me that my father and Engels, as socialists, betrayed their principles by hiring the services of a bourgeois detective. He recites passages from their writings ridiculing the institution of bourgeois marriage and calls upon me to remain true to socialist principles. His own previous bourgeois marriage, he says, should be a matter of no import to socialist comrades. He threatens that, if I leave, you too will suffer unfortunate consequences, that you are a hired medler and a police spy. He says he will follow me wherever I go, that my place is by his side, that together we can become a great force in the coming social revolution, that we should be an example to all the world of what a socialist couple can do, that our communion and church will be the socialist meeting hall where comrades assemble, and that our spirit will live in that of the socialist movement. He says he will cast aside secularism, that its work is done; all intelligent people are accepting Darwin, and Parliament and the universities have abolished religious requirements. Now the next item on the agenda is the socialist revolution. In that cause, he and I will share; our joint work will consecrate our lives. His eloquence, his idealism, and his great anger overwhelm me. I have no one to stand by my side, to strengthen me; and somehow he has discerned, Mr. Holmes, a great secret that I know concerning my father's personal life. He threatens to divulge it to the world socialist movement and to destroy the reputation of Karl Marx. That is his final weapon. I become unnerved, speechless.''

Holmes soothed Miss Marx. Then he said: "I think it would be best if you would go directly from here to your father's house without returning to the residence of Dr. Aveling. I can arrange myself to have all your belongings packed and delivered to you. But it would be most unwise for you to return to Dr. Aveling while he is engaged in threatening you in various ways. I shall speak with him instead. Let me assure you that after I have done so Dr. Aveling will not venture to repeat these threats to you."

"Shall I leave before this evening? I had been expecting to receive you and Irene Adler at Jews' Den."

"That would now be most unwise, Miss Marx."

"My few clothes and papers and books are now in one suitcase in my room. Please do bring them for me."

"We shall remember. Meanwhile, our first step will be to take you to your family's home."

Holmes and I drove with Eleanor Marx to her father's house. We spoke little on the way. Miss Marx said to Holmes once: "You are sure that you will secure Edward's assent to my departure and his promise to make no public statement against me or my father?"

"I can promise you, Miss Marx, that we shall succeed. I shall bring you a written statement from Dr. Aveling himself."

Holmes and I saw Eleanor Marx to her familial house. It stood sound and stolid in its brickstone; I still found it hard to conceive of it as the ganglion of the world's revolutionary movement. We did not, however, enter. Neither Holmes nor I would have cared to intrude upon or witness the scene of reunion between the daughter, and the ailing, tired revolutionist-father and the dying, worn-out mother.

I had expected that Holmes would ask the hansom cab to take us home. Instead, he called out our destination to the driver: "To Scotland Yard." I expressed my surprise. Holmes said that we were going to pick up a reinforcement, Detective Inspector Gibbon Lestrade himself, a tried and true practitioner of the science of criminal investigation, a trustworthy ally whom, as Holmes said, he had already informed of the essential details of the case. Within twenty minutes, we entered the austere precincts of Scotland Yard, experiencing an elation of security when we received the salute of its helmeted guards, who smiled as old friends to Mr. Sherlock

Holmes and then to the brown door, Room 202, otherwise unmarked, at which Holmes knocked. A pleasant baritone voice bade us enter, and Lestrade greeted us in friendly fashion.

"It's the Aveling-Marx case, I suppose," he said. "Has Aveling sprung any surprise?"

Holmes briefly told of Eleanor's arrival at our house, the threats of virtual blackmail that Aveling had made, and our own participation in Miss Marx's return to her father's house.

"A bad lot, these socialist revolutionaries, Mr. Holmes. We know so little about them. Do you know, Mr. Holmes, the Russian ambassador asked our prime minister, Mr. Gladstone, to keep an eye on these revolutionists, who otherwise might arouse the working class to revolution. Mr. Gladstone asked: 'Who is their leader?' The Russian ambassador said: 'A German Jew by the name of Karl Marx.' Mr. Gladstone replied laughingly: 'There is no chance that the British working class would follow a foreigner. No, we shall not place any of these anarchists or socialists under surveillance. Let them talk as much as they like, and publish their papers, so long as they perpetrate no deeds of outrage or violence.' "

We drove next to the house where Eleanor Marx had briefly set up her "Jews' Den."

"Of course," remarked Lestrade, "it should be clearly understood that Dr. Edward Aveling at this moment stands charged with no crime. That he is living with a young woman not his wife is no crime in the eyes of British law. That she has left her father and mother cannot, since she is in her mid-twenties, concern the law either. I am accompanying you, Mr. Holmes, solely as a friendly observer, without warrant, in case you do decide to make more serious charges."

Holmes nodded his head affirmatively: "I well understand, Lestrade, and I appreciate your readiness to stand by."

We soon knocked at the door of Aveling's flat. He opened the door, looked at us, unfriendly and without greeting, and then said: "I am much occupied at this time and cannot have callers."

Holmes said: "I am here on behalf of Miss Eleanor Marx to gather her belongings."

Aveling replied: "You have no right of entry here, and Miss Marx can speak for herself."

Holmes answered: "Perhaps you should also be told that I speak for little Jennie Burns of the Nell Gwynn and Thompson Street."

Aveling's face grew ashen; he stood uncertain, confused, shaken; then he visibly rallied his composure and without a word beckoned us to enter. The three of us entered his living room.

"Be seated, gentlemen," said Aveling. Then he added: "I fail to recognize the gentleman who accompanies you."

Holmes said: "I hurry to present Detective Inspector Gibbon Lestrade of Scotland Yard."

Lestrade interposed: "I wish to state, Dr. Aveling, that I am here without official warrant for entry and you are entirely free to ask me to leave."

After a momentary pause, Aveling responded: "You may stay, sir; I have violated no law and these gentlemen are meddling without reason in my personal affairs. Mr. Holmes has been interfering in the personal relations between myself and the young woman who is my wife in all but name only. Mr. Holmes is a paid agent of the infamous revolutionist and fomenter of violence Karl Marx, also a reputed spy in the service of Bismarck's secret police. Mr. Holmes takes his clients as they come, without regard to principle or honor, so long as he collects his fee. He violated British law to serve an Austrian prince; he simulated the dress of an Anglican minister, which is against the law, in order to burgle the flat of a young woman, Miss Irene Adler, which was also against the law. Mr. Holmes has the effrontery to come to my own house, to intimidate me through a threat of blackmail, all in the presence of a Scotland Yard inspector. Surely, Mr. Lestrade, the man you sit beside, Mr. Sherlock Holmes, is one you should arrest for his violation of the laws of England."

Lestrade slowly produced his pipe, filled it from a shaggy pouch; then, lighting it, he began to puff with some pleasure.

"Dr. Aveling," he said, "what you say is indeed most serious. My job is to enforce the laws of Britain against wrongdoers, whoever they are. You say that Mr. Holmes, simulating a clergyman's cloth, burgled the residence of a Miss Irene Adler. I cannot lay charges against Mr. Holmes unless the appropriate witness is forthcoming. Miss Adler has not made any complaint to the authorities, and I cannot act where no evidence exists. I presume there has been no external pressure on Miss Adler to withhold evidence; we would intervene to halt such influence if we had any ground to suspect its existence; and I have not heard Mr. Holmes engaging in any act of blackmail against yourself. If you wish to lay charges against Mr. Holmes, I shall be glad to have your written statement and shall take Mr. Holmes into custody at once for arraignment before a magistrate.''

Dr. Edward Aveling looked as desperate as any man I have seen. He looked from Holmes to Lestrade and myself, then quickly back again in reverse order, then tapered off to shorter oscillations, like the pendulum moving according to the Huygens' Principle I learned at school. As a physician I felt a twinge to see a person reduced to a pendular condition, albeit I knew that Holmes was acting with the highest sense of personal responsibility and honor. Dr. Aveling then asked in a husky voice: "What would you have me do, Mr. Holmes?''

"Would you address a letter to Miss Marx assuring her that you now agree with her entirely that it would be best for her to return to her father's house, that you will in no way try to prevent her continued residence there, and that you are granting me permission to remove a suitcase of her belongings from your own flat for delivery to Dr. Marx's house. Would you likewise add that you are writing this letter without constraint in the presence of myself, Dr. Watson, and Detective Inspector Lestrade.''

Without a further word, Dr. Aveling sat down at the table, took a sheet of paper, and wrote steadily for a few minutes. He gave the document to Holmes, who read it, pronounced it satisfactory, and handed it on for Lestrade and myself to read. It practically duplicated verbatim the text as Holmes had demanded it; evidently Aveling, in frightened panic at the mention of Jennie Burns's name, had preferred abject surrender to a probable prosecution and possible conviction for corrupting a child. Holmes thereupon placed the document in his coat pocket, went into a small side-room that served Miss Marx as a study, and returned with a suitcase; we all then left the Aveling flat. I felt as if I had been in a cavern where Evil was the presiding deity and Edward Aveling served as its chief votary.

We drove first to Scotland Yard to accommodate our good friend Lestrade.

"Without your imposing presence, Lestrade, we could never have secured that letter from Aveling. He is about as cunning and calculating a rascal as they come, but he had never counted on the intruding specter of poor little Jennie Burns."

"I surmised, Holmes," said Lestrade, "that you had a charge in the making of immorality with a child. They are terribly difficult charges to prosecute. The parents usually don't wish to see the case in court; sometimes they have behaved sordidly themselves. The child is fear-stricken perhaps to the point of being unable to speak coherently. The witnesses become vague and imprecise, and the magistrate scolds us for not preparing the case. But, thanks to you, we'll now keep our eyes on this Dr. Aveling."

We shook hands, and Lestrade walked vigorously into his fortress of justice.

"And now to Maitland Park Road to deliver the letter of release and the suitcase to Miss Marx, and we'll be off to tell Miss Irene Adler that our task is complete—that no rendezvous at the Aveling Flat will be necessary," cried Holmes.

The strain we had all been under was lessened. I could almost enjoy again the sight of London's humanity involved in its labors and relaxations, the busy streets, the endless houses, each doubtless with the strangest stories to tell. At the Marx residence, the aged Lenchen greeted us at the door with a smile that gave an unwonted cheerfulness to her dour face. She took us directly to the living room, where Eleanor Marx shortly joined us. Curiously, Miss Marx curtsied to Holmes and myself by way of greeting, as if to give a gestural seal to her renewed status as her father's daughter. Holmes presented her with the letter from Aveling, which she read twice with close attention.

"I am glad that Edward has been so considerate. You see, he is gentle and understanding after all. I am much needed here. My mother has but a few days more to live, and I hope her last days will be filled with understanding. The Moor too is sick; when he is able, he goes to the room of his Jenny von Westphalen and it's as if they were young lovers again in Triers. They joke about the love poems he has been sending her, and about her father, the kind Saint-

Simonian baron. Then he recites to her still another love poem he has written. All their four decades of misery, humiliation, and tragedy vanish for a half-hour, as if an unreal interlude had been dismissed and a beautiful new play were about to be written. Then they both become flushed and feverish and have to separate to different rooms."

There was a thrill to Miss Marx's voice, and I could see that it affected even Holmes, always protected though he was by a disciplined and analytical reason.

"We shall now proceed, Miss Marx," said Holmes after a pause, "to inform Miss Adler that there will happily be no need of a further meeting at Dr. Aveling's flat, that you are now restored to your father's house and taking care of your parents in their illness."

"Oh, I should like to go with you, Mr. Holmes, and tell Irene how admirably Edward has finally behaved. Lenchen can look after things while I'm gone for a short while."

Holmes bowed, and quickly Miss Marx placed a cloak over herself, said a few words to Lenchen, and accompanied us to a cab.

Chapter Ten

e climbed quickly to the flat of Miss Irene Adler. To our surprise, we were greeted by a small white envelope attached to the door and on it, writtern in letters drawn from newspaper articles: "TO MR. SHERLOCK HOLMES."

"Oh," said Eleanor Marx, "Irene has obviously had to go somewhere. But what a strange way to address a letter."

Holmes's face was stern. "That letter is not from Miss Adler," he said evenly. He tore it open, then showed us its page, in which another set of newspaper letters jostled each other like hieroglyphs:

> Tit for tat, Sherlock Holmes,
> To teach the bourgeois meddler.
>
> *From the Fighting Organization, Nechayev Group,*
> *International Workingmen's Alliance.*

Holmes's eyes became like telescope sights set against a searching mount. "There may be no time to lose. I must open this door at once," he said. He drew from his suit pocket a thin plate of steel, inserted it between the lock and door, pressing the bolt back, and swung the door open. He rushed through the corridor to the living room; there was still a slightly pungent smell of chloroform in the air, and the signs of a struggle that had taken place—pillows thrown askew, a reading lamp overturned, a chair thrown sideways. Miss Adler had kicked, struggled, and wrestled before she had been overcome.

Miss Marx stooped down and picked up from the floor a torn, ragged fragment of blue-red cashmere. "This was torn," she said "probably from the back of Irene's new dress. She had shown it to me last week and, when I asked her when she planned on wearing it, she answered, 'When I meet the man I love.' She was wearing it today."

Holmes said not a word. He was searching the floors, the furniture, the windows. "This was a simple kidnapping. She bit one of the men; here on the floor is a piece of the cotton gauze, soaked in chloroform, on which there is some blood; from the thumb mark on the gauze he was obviously right-handed, and quite determined in his intention. Another man held her down from behind. You can see that her necklace consequently was torn as he grasped her neck on its front jeweled side. They were obviously such single-minded kidnappers that they made no attempt to confiscate her necklace as booty. They did, however, open her desk where she kept her letters. Here is the box marked 'Letters,' but they are all gone. And another box marked 'Diaries'; they too are all gone. Evidently, this kidnapping was organized by someone who wished to accumulate as much private information about his victim and her friends as he possibly could—the windfall of the enterprise. Ah, here was where Miss Adler kept her funds; the boxes, however, are untouched, even those marked 'gilt-edged securities' and 'consols.' Here is another box of playbills and photographs; they too are undisturbed. No, our kidnapper is blatant about informing us that this was no act for petty criminal motives of larceny. Rather the aim in view was to paralyze my hand by proving to me that I too was vulnerable, that if I interfered in other people's personal lives they would simply strike against Irene Adler, as they could strike against you too, Watson. They would know that, however little I might prize my own life, I would be mortified by knowing that I had caused the death or injury of Irene, or allowed such to befall you, my dear Watson."

"My dear Holmes," I interrupted, "you need give yourself no anxiety on my account. I am an old campaigner, and I know the great battles of life are those wherein the alternative is death. We are aware that life is known at its highest only when fear is conquered.''

Eleanor Marx was meanwhile examining the letter closely. "Do you know what the 'Nechayev Group' could be, Mr. Holmes?'' she asked.

Holmes said he had read and heard of a Nechayev who led a criminal terrorist conspiracy in Russia, murdered a recusant, and was sentenced to life-imprisonment.

"That is all correct, Mr. Holmes. But there is much more to their bizarre story. Nechayev was a disciple of my father's great adversary, the anarchist Bakunin. Nechayev believed that the vocation of the revolutionist was to be a terrorist. Through deceit, theft, blackmail, betrayal, seduction, and murder, he believed the bourgeois system could be corrupted from within; then when it had grown putrescent to the core, it would be overthrown by a sanguinary uprising of the peasants led by the young intelligentsia, especially the students. The revolutionist, Nechayev insisted, was a doomed soul bound by an oath dedicating himself to destruction. Nechayev bore on his hands the scarred teeth-marks made by a student skeptic who had resisted as Nechayev throttled him to death. Nechayev's mind wove fantasies of an international society of conspirators, directed by an executive committee of which he was the supreme leader. Even old Bakunin finally repudiated this monomaniac. My father and his friends got hold of the facts about Nechayev's terrorist conspiracy and wrote a powerful exposé on behalf of the International Workingmen's Association. The anarchists then founded their own International Workingmen's Alliance.''

"And what has happened to Nechayev, meanwhile?''

"When last heard from, he was imprisoned in the Fortress of Peter and Paul in St. Petersburg and reportedly charming his jailers. But I had never heard of a Nechayev Section in England.''

"Obviously, Miss Marx, the writer of this letter not only knows of your present difficulties, but also admires the organizational methods and goals of Nechayev and Bakunin so much that he invents a section in whose name he is operating and proclaims the kidnapping of Irene Adler as a political blow against the doctrine of your anti-terrorist, authoritarian father. The criminal mentality during the next century will embellish itself increasingly in what your father calls ideology. I can think of only one man who has the determination and evil genius to pursue this devilish design in England. Meanwhile, we must get the help of Scotland Yard, tell them of all that has happened, and return you home, Miss Marx.''

I was most astonished by how calmly Miss Eleanor Marx acted and reasoned during this new unforeseen calamity. She responded with intellectual force and resourceful energy when the misfortunes of others were involved; these were external, objective events, with which she could cope forthrightly and realistically. It was only when the shadow of her father crossed her emotional existence that she became rebellious, hysterical, and flailed about in despair. What an amazingly gifted and charming woman she would have been, I thought, if her father's Jeremiah-like character had not dominated and twisted her earlier growth.

Once again we drove to Scotland Yard. Lestrade, having completed his day's work, was gone, but Inspector Stanley Hopkins took our report. He and Holmes set off together to Irene Adler's flat.

I did not see Holmes again till the following evening. He returned to our lodgings looking worried and exhausted.

"We have rarely had terrorists in England, Watson; there have been, to be sure, Fenian terrorists, but they were an alien force, hardly representative of the British character. Englishmen cannot be imagined sitting up nights to plot an assassination of a king or prime minister the way the Russians plotted the murder of their Czar. Can you imagine a student terrorist society founding itself at Oxford or Cambridge? But something seems to be changing. Those literary young men and women whom we met at William Morris's regard themselves as comrades of the Russian terrorists. They think of the Nihilists as negators of the existing system, much as Bernard Shaw does; but the negation ends there. Then they plan to run the whole new system as they direct, and the common people had better come along. Aveling and Moriarty are the precursors of a new academic species—the professors of revolution, who will regard the university as a breeding ground for revolutionists. The University of London will one day surpass the University of St. Petersburg for the training of revolutionists. The new species will dedicate itself

128

to the philosophy and technology of revolution; in their new theology the new friars will preach history's will and the mission to revolutionary self-abnegation.''

"But surely, Holmes, no one regards Aveling and Moriarty as typical of our new young scientists. May I inquire, however, whether you have advanced your investigation into the whereabouts of Miss Irene Adler? I should think that would be most on your mind.''

"It is, Watson. I have thought of nothing else these last twenty-four hours. I blame myself for having allowed Irene Adler to play a part in this case. I blame myself for having allowed my affections to permit her involvement when we were obviously dealing with men who think their genius exempts them from the moral law. I have enlisted all the Baker Street Irregulars, as well as their allies, the Whitechapel Mendozas, for full duty.''

"The Whitechapel Mendozas, Holmes? Who are they?''

"They're a group of very tough and hardened Jewish lads that came into existence when the anti-immigration agitators provoked riots in the East End. They call themselves after the renowned Jewish prizefighter, Daniel Mendoza, the champion of Britain and the father of scientific boxing, who a hundred years ago preferred pugilism to prayers as a way of persuading hoodlums. I have indeed prepared a new edition of his book *The Art of Boxing* that I have found invaluable. At any rate, I appealed to the Whitechapel Mendozas and told them that the life of Irene Adler is at stake.''

"And what precisely, Holmes, are they doing?''

"There's the usual eavesdropping and gossiping with the denizens of the criminal haunts, the inquiring among bartenders, barmaids, and informants for all suspicious circumstances and rumors of plans for kidnapping. Above all, they are maintaining a constant vigil at the house of Professor Robert Owen Moriarty, watching all comers and following them as well as Moriarty himself, so that we can trace on the map of London all the movements of the Moriarty gang.''

"But why Professor Moriarty, my dear Holmes?''

"Precisely because he's the only man in England who knew about Aveling, Eleanor Marx, Irene Adler, and myself in our inter-relations. I have no doubt that Aveling consulted with him and that the kidnapping was originally planned as a weapon to induce my withdrawal from the case of Eleanor Marx—an exchange of Irene Adler's freedom for the continued coresidence of Miss Marx with Dr. Aveling. Moriarty alone has the Bakuninist-terrorist approach to modern society; he has the logical intellect for solving the problems of organization and the knack for driving men. I had trouble finding his whereabouts. He had vanished into thin air, had stopped coaching at the University College, which had no idea where he lived.

"But Karl Pearson came to my rescue. Moriarty had once wanted to show him a theorem he had discovered in Lobachevskian geometry; he was so excited by his discovery that he invited Pearson, the only other man in London who would understand his proof, to visit him. Probably Moriarty now regrets that moment of sentimental scientific weakness, but it was all I needed. The Irregulars and the Mendozas are taking turns as sentinels, and Lestrade and Hopkins are considerately giving Scotland Yard's unofficial cooperation; they are not arresting our fellows as loiterers or peeping Toms. The inspectors had previously interrogated all the neighbors of Irene Adler. As I expected, they had heard no noise; but one had seen Miss Adler, who appeared to be ill, supported by two well-dressed men get into a hansom cab that then drove off. It took place about an hour before we arrived. And now we must await the word from our auxiliary detachments; I hope that comes before we have to start daily searches of the newspapers' agony columns."

"What would her kidnappers now demand?" I queried, much puzzled.

"I can only conjecture, Watson. Possibly some money from Engels, possibly an added commitment from me to withdraw from my profession as a detective. I would be a kind of prisoner on parole. Sooner or later the terrorists are bound to discover that kidnapping hostages is far more lucrative than assassinations. It requires, however, a considerable measure of organization to house and guard the victim and to secure the extorted funds. But I dare say the imagination of Professor Moriarty is superb on such matters."

I was aware from Holmes's firmly held tense face and the level

tone of his conversation to what degree the kidnapping of Irene
Adler was taxing the limits of his self-control. He seemed to be trying to restrain all his anger against the perpetrator lest it warp the
clarity of his reasoning. Deeply as his feelings were involved with
Irene Adler, he struggled all the more to maintain an appearance of
detachment and the calmness of the purely analytical observer. He
seemed to encourage digressive conversation for the effect that its
sheer irrelevance had in quieting his nerves. He sat there an
embodiment of potential energy, a tightly drawn spring waiting for
the signal to act. I offered him a newly published novel by a writer
called Thomas Hardy that had stirred me greatly with its honest
portraiture of human nature, its love for the English countryside,
and its unswerving pessimism in philosophy. Holmes thanked me,
saying that what he had heard of Hardy made him think that they
had much in common but that he could not at the moment bring his
attention to bear on a work of art.

I feared greatly that Holmes might have recourse again to the
drug that he had, partially in response to my prodding, renounced.
I am sure the thought crossed his mind. Wherefore I turned to him,
and said: "Forgive me, my dear Holmes, if I presume on our
friendship. But I well realize the strain that the recent events have
imposed on your constitution. I know how deeply attached you are
to the person and welfare of Miss Irene Adler, and how profound
your distress at her present danger. I also knew however that you
are doing all that intelligence and work can do to bring her home
safely, and to apprehend her criminal captors. I would say too that
you would not spare your life to achieve her safety. I think Miss
Adler would say that she feels proud to have evoked such a regard
from Sherlock Holmes."

Holmes looked into the fireplace for a few seconds and then
said: "Your words mean more to me than I can say, Watson."

Then he took down from the bookcase his *Index of Random
Items,* and remarked: "Have you ever observed, my dear Watson,
that in a time of stress nothing is more comforting than to peruse
an encyclopaedia, or an almanac? You just sit back and absorb a
flow of facts; you simply collect information. It must appeal to
something primordial in our characters. The Darwinists say that
our primal ancestors were collectors, food-gatherers; they picked

up nuts, plants, berries, vegetables, fruits wherever they could. The more they collected and stored, the more secure they felt. Perhaps a collector's instinct is deeply ingrained in us. Have you noticed, Watson, that every child, if allowed to, will make a collection of something, seashells, birds' eggs, matchboxes? I myself used to collect birds, and I mastered enough taxidermy to make our house look like an aviary; my father was content with his butterflies, and even my mother cultivated a collection of mushrooms. What about you, Watson?"

"I did collect pebbles when I was a child."

"How curious! I wonder if any psychologist has tried to explain the principle underlying our choices for collecting."

"I have never heard of any, though I should think there would be too many chance factors to allow for a coherent theory."

Once again there was a knock at our door, and Mrs. Hudson ushered in two young lads of about thirteen years each. Holmes leaped up animatedly, saying: "Watson, may I present to you Sean Thomas, chief runner of the Baker Street Irregulars, and Moshe Shinwell of the Whitechapel Mendozas."

I shook hands with them formally as both of them grinned at me. "You're a doctor, are you really?" asked Sean Thomas. I nodded assent.

"I'd like to become one myself, when I finish at the Jews' School," said Moshe Shinwell.

"Now tell me, lads, what have you learned?" asked Holmes.

"He's a shifty one, that professor," said Sean Thomas. "At five-twenty o'clock the professor left his house as if to take a walk. Moshe and I followed along like two sniffing dogs. He moved round and round; once maybe he saw us, but thought we were just two boys, loafers. Then he moved up Thomas More Lane and right into the church. Moshe and I followed along inside, though Moshe didn't like to go."

"I just became a bar mitzvah last month, and I promised my mother and father at my speech in the school that I'd be a good Jew."

"I well understand, Moshe. I myself have felt a certain qualm at entering a mosque," said Holmes. Holmes turned to me and remarked: "The vicar of the church at Thomas More Lane is the

Reverend Hewlett, who is well known for sermons that argue that anarchism is the new Christianity.''

Sean Thomas continued: ''We sat down quietly in a side seat at the back next to an old lady who sat like in the dark with her head bent and looking sadly. Then we could see the professor stand near a tall man sitting on the left side; he got up and walked along with the professor to the entrance hall. Moshe and I slipped through a side door where we could watch them from the stairs. They talked quietly for about ten minutes. Then the professor left first. I told Moshe I'd follow him, and that he should follow the tall man. I moved right along. The professor went roundabout again, but stopped along some fruit stalls to buy apples, pears, and cherries. Then he went to his house and opened his door with a key. My relief came in at that time, and I headed here and met Moshe getting here at the same time.''

''And you, Moshe?''

''The big man walked fast toward the waterfront. He turned at Castlereagh Place off Shipyard Street; I got there in time to see him open a door with a key to a battered old two-story building, Number 18, whose windows were boarded up and that looked deserted, as if no one looked after it anymore. There was a painted sign that said: 'Small Machines and Equipment, Ltd.' I could see no light in any of the front windows. I waited for a while, then decided I'd better get back to you, Mr. Holmes.''

''That's fine, Moshe. Now, I have a letter I wish you and Sean would take to Inspector Lestrade at Scotland yard.'' Holmes quickly wrote a few lines that he sealed in an envelope and addressed to Gibbon Lestrade. The two lads saluted and departed briskly. Then Holmes turned to me; his eyes seemed kindled as if by flames darting from deep within him.

''I fear there will be danger tonight. We are dealing with villains who will stop at nothing, who kidnap a woman and would as soon leave her dead. Moreover, they are embrazened by the knowledge that an organization stands behind them. They can consult with Professor Moriarty, whose intellect, solving all problems, must be a perpetual astonishment to them. The Small Machines and Equipment, Ltd., was founded by anarchist and nihilist friends in England as a convenient purchasing and export center for firearms and explosives for their comrades on the continent. Probably their space is available to Professor Moriarty and his henchmen with no questions asked and no information required. The petty criminal minds are now transfigured by a philosophic and ideological consciousness. Therefore, I suggest, Watson, you accompany yourself with the Woolwich revolver that served as your sidearm in the Afghan War. Please do make sure that each chamber has a bullet. As for myself, this newly arrived Colt firearm, with its unusual rotating momentum and accuracy in aim, will, I hope, stand me in good stead.''

We were soon in a hansom cab driving to Castlereagh Place and Shipyard Street. The cabman muttered to us hoarsely that he did not like to leave two such fine gentlemen alone in such a wretched neighborhood. He asked us whether we were sure that we hadn't made a mistake in the address. Holmes assured him there was none. He then walked slowly toward No. 18, and I went quietly with him. He observed the location of the house carefully. "It was forty-two steps from the intersection," said Holmes. "Now let's go to the street behind and see if we can find access to the building."

We proceeded to Shipyard Street and went on to the next side-street, called Horatio Place. It was even drabber than Castlereagh Place, if that were imaginable—a series of decaying old buildings that seemed to be used for petty storage, dubious shops, and a virtual Rochdale cooperative for rodents. Holmes carefully walked forty-two steps down Horatio Place. To our right stood a three-story structure for some sheet-metal shops.

"Excellent," said Holmes. The door fortunately was open. "Evidently the fear of burglars was felt to be here, in Jeremy Bentham's word, minimized," he remarked. We entered the house and climbed its three floors; the stairway then opened after a short stairwell onto the roof. Through the maze of chimneys we wended our way to peer over the roof-ledge on the back side of No. 18, Castlereagh Place. Between the boards of one window we could see a flickering light.

"That's probably where her jailers keep guard," said Holmes, "and Irene is probably kept prisoner in an adjoining room that has no window at all, but, at most, an airshaft. These old buildings were constructed in an age that did not value fresh air and light and prized more the saving in fuel.'' He studied the adjoining structures, their contours and accesses, like a field commander reconnoitering the enemy outposts. ''If we go down the old fire-escape here,'' said Holmes, ''we can reach across to the roof of 18 Castlereagh.''

The rusted steps of the fire escape creaked in painful protest as we descended them. Probably they had known no human foot in half a century. Then Holmes stepped onto the roof of 18 Castlereagh, and I did likewise. We went as noiselessly as we could and slowly to the roof door. It was closed with a small wire-latch from the inside. Holmes produced his thin steel ruler from his pocket, gently lifted the latch, and we entered the stairwell. As quietly as we could we descended the stairs to the second story of the dingy house; the wooden planks creaked under our feet. But we trusted that any listener would take them to be the rats of the district in their journeys to and fro. The dimmest of gas lights between the first and second floors gave us just enough glimmer of light so that we saw the outlines of our bodies, but nothing more.

Then we heard voices coming through a wooden door. We strained our ears. One coarse, leering voice was speaking: ''I said to the chief, 'Now that we has got her for a while, in our power, let us handle her as we will.' The chief said: 'Maybe later but not just yet. That would break her spirit. We may want her to write a letter to her detective admirer. If we use her now, we could never get her to write the kind of letter we'd want. And with a letter from her, and his heightened fear, we shall be able to call his tune. Afterwards— the free untrammeled revolt of sexual passion,' he says, 'is part of the passion for revolution itself.' He's a funny one, the chief; he talks like a book, but what book in a library could ever have told us: 'Boys, the woman is all yours.' ''

I could hear Holmes's breath deep with anger. These lowest, most savage, most bestial of criminals, were finding their spokesman in this twisted-minded professor of mathematics who called himself a Bakuninist-Marxist.

Then a second voice responded: ''I tell you, Verne, if you'd listen to the chief long enough and then copy it down, you could write a book. No one has ever been able to command the gangs like the way he does. He knows more law than the lawyers, more about guns than the gunsmiths, and has maps for every street in London. You should see him studying how to do a bank, checking every-thing, the time, the money, the police, the tellers. All you have to do is follow his A, B, C, D, and it's like he was our engineer. And he's as fair as they come in dividing up the loot and handing out the jobs, but you get for as much as you did, with a percentage natural-ly going to the organization. I feel a lot better since I signed on with him.''

There was a pause. The first asked the second with revolting obscenities whether the woman in the adjoining room was getting restless. The reply came, "She's getting restless."

And indeed, through the two doors, we could hear the second joking to the first: "Guess she wants your company to the toilet."

The first answered, "All right, Del, I'll go to her. The place stinks enough already."

We heard him walking, then working at unlocking a heavy chain and pushing a clumsy, jarring door open.

Holmes produced his revolver. "Now is our time, Watson. Have your firearm ready."

He pushed the lock of the door to enter. It did not yield. He fired one bullet into the mechanism and, throwing his whole weight onto the door, thrust it open. "You're under arrest," he shouted.

There in an adjoining chamber we could see Irene Adler, with hands bound but standing, and next to her, reaching confusedly for his gun, the man whom we now knew as Verne.

The scoundrel clasped Irene, and held her in front of him as a shield. "Drop your weapon," he shouted at Holmes.

Holmes hesitated for a moment and the kidnapper, holding Irene with his left arm, raised his right arm to aim at Holmes. At that instant, Irene Adler hurled herself with the most violent force at his right arm, and as she fell the criminal's gun fired. Then Holmes, aiming with precision, fired at the man's heart. Mean-while, the second man, Del, recovering from his bewilderment was cocking a revolver at Holmes. I could not delay, and I fired at him from the side, even as he fired simultaneously.

The partially lit room, poorly ventilated, was heavy with the smell and texture of smoke. The noise of the guns in this small space had been deafening. And now, too, I could smell as well human blood flowing from three fallen bodies. Holmes and I rushed to Irene Adler; she was unconscious, and blood was oozing from a wound high in her back. I stanched it with my handkerchief as best I could, and said: "We must get her at once to Bart's; there's no time to lose."

We began carrying Irene's limp body through the dark rooms toward the stairway, when we heard the steps of several men resounding upwards. There appeared like a spirit in the smoke taking physical form the welcome face of Inspector Lestrade, and behind him the vague silhouettes of two helmeted constables bearing lanterns.

"I heard shots as we arrived, Holmes. What's happened?"

Briefly, Holmes told how the kidnapper had shot Irene Adler and how we had fired as well. Only then I noticed that Holmes's left shoulder was drenched in blood; in our excitement we had not noticed he had been struck by a bullet. A constable took hold of Irene's body, as Holmes began staggering; Lestrade lent a hand to Holmes and the second constable guided us down the stairs. An image crossed my mind of a Shakespearean play I had seen in which Sir Henry Irving acted; to the "exeunt" of Shakespeare's script, the last scene was of fallen bodies being carried out in a general pell-mell.

In Lestrade's police cab, we conveyed the now partially conscious Irene Adler and the wounded Holmes to St. Bartholomew's Hospital. Miss Adler's wound proved very serious, indeed. The bullet had traversed her body near the heart and, completing its route from back to front, left no cartridge behind. The blood flow was stanched and surgeons closed her tissues. Holmes too had finally collapsed from loss of blood; the bullet was extracted from near his clavicular bone, and for a few days he was in a high fever. Lestrade interrogated me closely in the early hours of the morning. He had been late in receiving Holmes's message because other duties had taken him outside Scotland Yard. He responded at once to Holmes's plea for assistance; Holmes had written that he believed Irene Adler was held prisoner in No. 18, Castlereagh Place, by at least two men, that he feared danger to her life and safety, and that therefore he and I were going to try to rescue her; he hoped the inspector and constables would arrive to seize the malefactors, and if need be, assist us both as well.

I told Lestrade of all that Holmes had learned from his youthful aides, Sean Thomas and Moshe Shinwell. Lestrade doubted that an encounter in the Reverend Hewlett's Labor Church was sufficient ground for a warrant of arrest against Professor Moriarty, but that, in any case, he would place him under surveillance and question him directly after the identities of the two dead kidnappers were definitely ascertained. That was accomplished within a few hours; the large, tall man whom Holmes had shot was a dissolute, pretentious man known as Verne "Venomous," associated much with a group of exiled French Blanquists; they spent a large part of their free time compiling lists of persons they would execute when they took power and quarreling with Karl Marx. "Venomous" made his living through petty extortions from aged Jewish storekeepers in Whitechapel, whom he called "Rothschilds" and threatened with anti-Semitic epithets. The other, Del Larkson, a wizened Australian disciple of Edward Carpenter's cult of sexuality, wrote leaflets propagandizing that the new revolutionary vandals would be practitioners of his sexual creed; this was the sick, wretched man I had slain.

Chapter Eleven

everal hours later the afternoon newspapers bore headlines telling of the rescue of the noted former operatic singer Irene Adler from her kidnappers. It told of the exchange of fire between the kidnappers and Holmes and his colleague Dr. Watson. Photographs of the dingy building at 18 Castlereagh Lane were on the front page, and also pictures of Irene Adler in all her operatic splendor. The articles were on the whole accurate, with their description of Holmes firing after "Venomqus" had almost killed Miss Adler. The backgrounds of the kidnappers were described at length; the question was raised whether the colonies of terrorists in London—French, Russian, Italian, German—should be kept under strict surveillance or whether indeed persons committed to the ethic and practice of terrorism merited the right of political asylum in Britain. I turned from all these articles with distaste. For the first time, Sherlock Holmes had taken the life of another person, albeit to defend his own and that of Irene Adler. And I, a physician, sworn by oath to be a healer of men's illnesses, had inflicted death, yet had no moral compunctions concerning what I had done. I could now however also understand why among primitive folk the warrior, returned from battle, does penance for the life he has taken and asks its shade to trouble him not in this world.

Meanwhile, Irene Adler's survival continued to remain uncertain. Gradually, however, she began to improve. The turning point came one day, I think, when Holmes, who was regaining his strength, asked me to assist him while he ventured forth for a social call on Miss Irene Adler. He was still in the hospital garments, but he got permission to wear his cap and pipe. We walked with smallish steps through corridors and down stairs and turned into Irene's room. She was lying flat, on a low pillow, with a novel propped in her two hands—Jane Austen's *Northanger Abbey.* She laughed like a schoolgirl when she saw Holmes, and for a few minutes I deemed it proper, as a doctor, to leave the two patients alone.

There were visitors too who came by to cheer Holmes. Inspector Lestrade called and told Holmes that Professor Moriarty had dropped out of sight completely before he could be questioned, having vanished from the house he had rented and never appearing again to coach his college students. He still found it hard to believe that an eccentric mathematician might become the first chief in London of a criminal organization, but he was obviously concerned by a new informed managerial aggressiveness in London's criminal circles.

Then one day, the old and sick Karl Marx, accompanied by his jaunty ex-cavalryman, Frederick Engels, came to see Holmes to express his good wishes. I chanced to be there that afternoon and I shall not forget how Dr. Marx was filled with genuine good humor and concern for Holmes. Engels left us for a while as he went to pay his respects to Irene Adler. Marx told Holmes that it was fitting that he had exchanged shots to liberate a woman such as Irene Adler from a Bakuninist lumpen-proletarian. Marx amused Holmes immensely by telling him that he approved of duels if they were fought over exceptional questions of honor and that, since among communist comrades such challenges were frequent, he used to practice fencing and pistol-shooting in a French communist fencing salon on Oxford Street. One of his fencing partners attained a certain notoriety when he was later hanged as a murderer. Marx felt that there would be a lot less irresponsible slander in newspapers if English law permitted duels. He might have done some dueling himself, but one had to take a boat to Belgium; and he thought a rough channel crossing, compounded with seasickness, took the fun out of maiming some class enemy with a pistol-ball.

Marx also presented Holmes with his book *Das Kapital* as a

mark of gratitude to the detective. On the flyleaf, Marx inscribed in as careful a handwriting he could contrive from his misshapen, uneven, crabbed letters: "To my celebrated young friend, Sherlock Holmes: May this inquiry into the bourgeois economy be taken as a sign of my esteem for your heroic example in the struggle against human oppression."

Holmes thanked Marx warmly: "I have at the moment at Baker Street a copy of only one of my brochures, that on the types of tobacco ash, to offer you in return, but it is scarcely a work of theoretical import. I am planning however to write a study of the means society can take to withstand the novel evolution of organized crime and terrorism that Professor Robert Owen Moriarty now not only envisages but evidently plans to practice. When it is done, I shall be pleased to send you a copy."

Marx thanked Holmes beamingly. He told Holmes that his daughter Eleanor was busily at work translating another play by Ibsen; he dared hoped she would turn soon to writing of her own, or better still, marry some young man like the gifted Charles Waldstein. "I should hate to see my Tussy, my last daughter, married to a husband in another country, even another town. As I get older, my family matters more to me than all the historical movements."

Holmes replied that he could well understand that. The two old men, Marx and Engels, then left, waving their hands in farewell.

Holmes watched them sadly, and said: "When Marx dies, his daughter Eleanor will turn to Edward Aveling as sure as the fog comes to London. Those Ibsen plays tell her own life. Somehow the sins of the fathers are visited on the children; it's the way of life itself and mitigated only by the fact that their virtues too can be transmitted and inherited. Men like Marx who have made a fetish of revolution impose a debilitating burden on their children. They leave them suspicious, cantankerous, and, above all, deprived of a joy in life for itself; the children lack the mainstay of a code built around decency, respect for others, love for work. There is something hollow, even bogus, in professing that human beings cannot live worthwhile lives without committing themselves to a grandiose philosophy of history; the rickety, scholastic foundation can collapse so easily. Learned scholars are too often weavers of fantasy that they punctuate with footnotes; however, fantasies are precisely what sick people want to hear."

Eleanor Marx indeed soon began to visit Irene Adler almost daily. She would read to her from the manuscript of the new translation she was working on, a play by Ibsen called *Ghosts.* The two women thought this was the most daring play ever written, touching on a problem that had never before been made the subject of a drama. Irene Adler, from her large theatrical experience, doubted that any English producer would dare risk his capital or good name to stage such a play. She said Bernard Shaw was going around calling himself an Ibsenite and lecturing to whomsoever would listen on the quintessence of Ibsenism; two days previously he actually had made Ibsen the subject of a lecture from a platform in Hyde Park. One of the seedy onlookers interrupted and shouted: "Hey, gov'nor, why do you talk about a bloody Scandinavian? Why don't you talk about a good Englishman like Shakespeare?"

Shaw replied with a gracious smile: "My dear fellow, Ibsen knows far more than Shakespeare ever did; Shakespeare lived before Newton, Darwin, and Karl Marx; Ibsen has had the benefit of all three. And Shakespeare himself wrote a play about a Scandinavian prince—*Hamlet*—and it's his greatest."

Eleanor Marx, however, preferred to make only a very brief call of courtesy upon Sherlock Holmes. She obviously felt a certain resentment that he had come between her and Edward Aveling and still rejected any conception of the recesses of Aveling's depravity.

Holmes remarked: "To convince her I should have to take her to the Nell Gwynn to talk intimately with little Jennie Burns. Even then she might disbelieve or think this was purchased testimony, manufactured by Edward's enemies. And if she did believe the evidence, her nerves might break under the strain, and her own tenuous clutch to sanity, or life itself, might be severed." Holmes therefore hoped that her own advancing experience and confidence might bring her good judgment, but I could see that he apprehended the makings of a lifelong tragedy.

Finally, after several weeks, Irene Adler was recovered enough to leave St. Bartholomew's Hospital. Holmes was already his old self at Baker Street. Irene decided that she wished to complete her convalescence by resting at an inn frequented mainly by actors and located in Cornwall, called The Cornish Queen. She and Holmes arranged to go together, and I too spent a weekend with them. They talked so much and endlessly together that I would warn her to desist and rest. Irene liked to talk about books she had read, people she had met, places she had seen; Holmes would ask her all sorts of questions. Then Irene would query him about his cases; her evident sincere and affectionate interest seemed to breach his customary reserve; the man whom I knew as naturally incommunicative seemed to have regained a lost eloquence.

Several weeks thus went by, and one day Holmes returned to Baker Street. His face had a healthy ruddy tinge and he was obviously cheerful at the prospect of resuming work. I presented him with the list of persons who had called to see him during his absence. Mrs. Hudson and I had been careful in keeping such a record. I asked after Miss Adler.

Holmes replied directly. "Irene Adler is starting to pack her effects. In a fortnight, she is returning to the United States, her native country."

I expressed my surprise at this decision, and gently hinted that I thought she and Holmes might draw their lives together.

Holmes again answered directly. "Irene sees clearly that a married bond between us would terminate my own work as a consulting detective, as it would her own efforts at social alleviation. She asks me: 'How would you feel free to depart for your investigations at strange hours, be absent for days or weeks on end without being able to inform me of your whereabouts?' She would fret and worry for my safety, and willy-nilly wish to see me engaged in work less dangerous and less onerous. Inevitably, she feels that out of consideration for her I would begin to withdraw from taking precisely those kinds of cases where my powers have most manifested themselves. Finally, as my practice became humdrum, I would abandon it altogether. On her own side, Irene feels that she cannot pursue the vocation of a settlement worker without herself living at the settlement house and sharing, to that extent, the life of the poor in the neighborhood. That is her calling, and I do not think that I should try to dissuade her. I can see all the hazards in being the wife of a consulting detective; the Moriarty's of the world are in full offensive. The kidnapping ordeal still remains in Irene's memory, as a warning foretaste perhaps of bitter experiences in a life joined with mine. Would our children ever know the tranquility of their parents' untroubled affection? Therefore, my dear Watson, I shall go to Southampton to see Irene embark for America. You are most welcome to join me, if you wish."

I replied that I would be happy to say Godspeed to Miss Adler at Waterloo Station, but could not leave the experiments on dengue fever cultures in which I was engaged at the Section for Tropical Disease. Holmes, without further ado, began discussing these experiments with me.

Thus Holmes took up again his practice as a consulting detective. The rescue of the former operatic star Irene Adler had made his name a household word on the continent as well as in Britain. His astuteness and courage in confronting the anarchist kidnappers were celebrated among princes and commoners, monarchists, liberals, and socialists alike. The number of cases, actual and potential, increased to such an extent that Holmes henceforth with much regret could select only a few for his attention. Happily, the young chiefs of the Baker Street Irregulars and the Whitechapel Mendozas under Holmes's tutelage later coalesced their associates as the Baker Street Regulars, and provided help especially to the London working and lower-middle classes, achieving an enviable record as an investigative agency. But the genius of Holmes's intuitive penetration was something that could not be transmitted.

I shall treasure the memory of my last meeting with Irene Adler. An assemblage of friends cheered her as she prepared to board the Southampton Boat Express at Waterloo Station. Eleanor Marx, Amy Levy, Bernard Shaw, Olive Schreiner, May Morris—the whole young literary world was there. Miss Marx was weeping. Amy Levy recited a poem that had as *envoi* the French proverb: *Partir, c'est mourir un peu.*

Bernard Shaw declared that now that Irene Adler had renounced the operatic stage he would probably renounce musical criticism altogether and write socialist plays exclusively. "All the women I love always give me up," he announced. "I shall finally have to marry a woman I do not love."

"Everybody laughed, though I must acknowledge I found his humor distasteful. Irene Adler admonished me to remain the good friend of Sherlock Holmes and thanked me warmly for my part in having helped rescue her at such a risk to my own life. She invited me to be her guest in the United States in case I should ever visit her country, to which I responded that I hoped to do so someday.

Then the train left with Irene Adler waving to us with two flags, one British, the other American—a picture of joyous energy such as I have never seen before; and Holmes, from the adjoining window in the same compartment, watching her with a broader smile than I had ever observed on his face.

Holmes returned to Baker Street by next morning's early boat train. He plunged into his cases with a zeal that was unprecedented. There was now a species of fanaticism in his work. It was clear that the kidnapping and near-killing of Irene Adler were critical events in his personal life. He was no longer the detached student of crime, the pure scientist observing the criminal type, and taking more delight in solving the mysteries of crimes purely as intellectual problems than in the aim for justice. Henceforth, there was something of the personal vendetta in his work. He kept alert for those crimes organized in a masterly way that bore the stamp of Professor Moriarty's genius; he distinguished between the conventional cases and those that were "criminally mathematical." He had a physical hatred for Moriarty as a man who would have had Irene Adler murdered or personally humiliated. It seemed never completely to leave his consciousness. Sometimes he discussed it with me on a more generalized and philosophical level.

"My dear Watson, the criminal mentality and the scientific mind have hitherto in the course of history rarely been combined in the same person. To be sure, Francis Bacon, the protagonist of modern science, was convicted by the king's court of accepting bribes while serving as Lord Chancellor; but Bacon, though a great philosopher, was not a scientist. I can think of none from Newton to Darwin or Descartes or Pasteur who showed criminal tendencies. But as Darwin and Wallace have taught us, the tendency to variation is a zoological universal. The destructive, criminal variation has now evidently begun to appear among those with scientific intelligence. The variation may spread, passing the test of the struggle for existence and making, through natural and social selection, for the origin of a new subspecies, that of scientific men who take pleasure in the destruction of humanity. Perhaps the benighted and ignorant medieval peasants who hated the person of the alchemist Dr. Faustus had a strange intimation that an uncontrollable destructive force was being engendered in his workshop of retorts, tubes, scales, and liquids boiling to spew their fumes.''

"I pray, Holmes that such persons will be seized and executed or incarcerated and that such a subspecies will be rendered extinct long before it can inflict its damage."

"The difficulty is, Watson, that the scientific powers of the criminally scientific will make them esteemed in the eyes of mankind. They will create marvels of technology, and mankind may well be proud of them. But they will not wish mankind well and may as leave see it extirpated from the earth."

"But surely, my dear Holmes, no species in evolutionary history has done such violence to itself. It is inconceivable that the human species should be the first to become so self-destructive."

"Who knows, Watson, whether some species may have driven themselves to their own eradication?"

I felt that Holmes almost pictured himself as waging a personal combat against the forces of human self-destruction exemplified by Professor Moriarty. When later that combat was finally realized in a personal battle that ended with Moriarty's death, I told part of the story, but part only. I could not during the lifetime of any of Marx's immediate family write about the circumstances of the case of Eleanor Marx that first brought Professor Moriarty to Holmes's notice.

Postscriptum

uring the seventeen years from 1881 to 1898, I watched the socialists gaining in influence; the Fabian Society caught the mood of young Britons eager for a more humane world, and Bernard Shaw was becoming the most talked about playwright, who had elevated lowly social problems onto the art of the stage. Karl Marx seemed to have become the prophet of a new religion among European working-men, Russian Nihilists, and Scottish Calvinist and English Methodist preachers. I could never feel much respect for Marx, the new prophet; I had seen him at too close quarters, a bewildered old man clutching his dreams; he resembled too much the atheistical man of letters whom our celebrated Edmund Burke had depicted during the French Revolution constructing their political schemes like *a priori* geometers. Then it happened one day that our remembrances of Marx and his unhappy daughter were revived most poignantly.

On a chilly Saturday morning, April 2, 1898, Holmes had set the fire blazing and we were enjoying the breakfast of fried eggs, oats, and cream that Mrs. Hudson had prepared for us. Holmes remarked that he had fallen asleep the previous night while trying to read a novel entitled *Madame Bovary*.

"I found it boring," he remarked, "though its introduction was most enjoyable. You will be surprised to know that the translator was none other than our acquaintance of years past, Eleanor Marx; she now signs herself 'Eleanor Marx-Aveling.'"

"Alas, Holmes," I responded, "then she must have married the scoundrel."

"Perhaps, my dear Watson. The translator's introduction, however, is so eloquent concerning the heroine's search for an ideal that I wondered whether the translator's own search for her ideal had failed her. *Madame Bovary,* though it ends in suicide, seems to be Eleanor Marx's own personal manifesto."

"Is there any socialism or communism in her introduction, Holmes?" I asked, pleased that my friend was turning to literature.

"My dear Watson," Holmes answered, "you address me as if I were a literary critic, a species of men of letters that I find as repugnant as John Keats did. I should have every criticism preceded by a short summary of the author's previous judgments, the failures as well as successes; then we might be spared pronouncements that are more pretending to omniscience than the latest papal bull. But, no, Miss Marx never quite suggests that Madame Bovary would have been happier in a socialist society. Perhaps her experience with Edward Aveling began slowly to teach her that a socialist society will not transmute human evil into good, and that the Edward Avelings of the world who flourish abundantly in our present socialist enclaves may, perhaps, do even more so in future socialist orders."

At this moment Mrs. Hudson's gentle knock at the door intervened; she entered bearing the day's morning newspapers. Gravely she placed them on the small table next to Holmes's easy chair. Holmes rose, picked up the newspaper, turned a page or so, and then, for a moment, stood silent. He read intently for a few minutes, then handed me the newspaper opened to the offending page and sank into his chair pensively.

I too was shocked as I read the headline: "Eleanor Marx Aveling, Daughter of the Revolutionist Karl Marx, Commits Suicide." An article of two columns followed. Eleanor Marx, it transpired, had on the morning of Thursday, March 31st, at her residence in Jews' Walk, Sydenham, received a letter that much upset her; subsequently she sent her maid to the nearest chemist's shop with an identifying card in the name of Dr. Edward Aveling, her husband, and a note stating: "Please give bearer chloroform and small quantity prussic acid for dog. E.A." Shortly thereafter the maid returned with a small package, together with the chemist's ledger notebook that all persons receiving a poisonous drug are obliged to sign. Mrs. Aveling took the notebook into the front room where Mr. Aveling was occupied and then returned with the signature "E. M. Aveling."

It was then a few minutes after ten o'clock; Dr. Aveling announced he was leaving for "uptown"; Mrs. Aveling pleaded that he remain at home because of his recent illness. Nevertheless, he left. Dr. Aveling then proceeded to the headquarters of the Social Democratic Federation, where he spent the day with several comrades writing a pamphlet for their forthcoming annual May Day demonstration. Mrs. Aveling meanwhile wrote three letters, one to her solicitor, one to her husband, Dr. Aveling, and another to her nephew in France. Then, as her maid attests, she took a bath, dressed herself in white, and retired to bed. When her maid, entering the room a few minutes later, found her unconscious, she hurried to a neighboring doctor for help, but Mrs. Aveling was dead by the time the doctor arrived.

Mrs. Aveling, the article concluded, was well known in the trades-union movement, especially for her work in the Gasworkers and General Labourers Union; she was also much admired for her dramatic and poetic recitations before the Shelley Society and Socialist League, and for her vigorous articles in socialist, labor, and freethinking periodicals. Above all she was much respected for her literary work, in particular for her translations of Henrik Ibsen's plays from the Norwegian originals and of Gustave Flaubert's notorious novel *Madame Bovary,* which had elicited a prosecution in France under the Bonapartist Empire. Mrs. Aveling died childless.

"Good God! Holmes!" I cried. "We had just been talking of this poor unfortunate and unhappy woman!"

Holmes's eyes seemed listless, and his mind seemed elsewhere, as on some distant journey.

"The novel ended that way too," he said, "with the heroine dying from the poison she had imbibed; she too wrote a letter, and dressed in white like a bride."

"She ordered the poison herself, Holmes, with her husband in the front room. How callous and unfeeling could Edward Aveling be."

"If she ordered it herself, Watson, it was in a manner of speaking. Eleanor Marx signed herself 'E.M.A.,' but the request for the poison was signed 'E.A.,' the initials of Edward Aveling. Conceivably Aveling might have signed it himself. The receipt, however, was in Eleanor Marx Aveling's name. Either way, Edward Aveling seems to have been privy to his wife's procurement of the poison. Did the Avelings indeed own a sick, ailing dog? The article says nothing about an animal in the household. With the professional card of Dr. Edward Aveling accompanying the request, the chemist probably took the 'Dr.' as signifying a doctorate of medicine; very few Londoners would even know that there is such a degree as a 'Doctor of Science.' But I shall say no more. We can invent hypotheses; we can conjecture; but, as Professor William Stanley Jevons has written in his admirable *Principles of Science,* facts are required to eliminate hypotheses and every fact is a crucial experiment among rival hypotheses."

I had often observed in my friend Sherlock Holmes that, whenever a situation of emotional stress presented itself, he would as a means for reasserting his own powerful self-control assume an almost professorial guise. At such moments, he would allow himself to refer to recondite treatises or monographs that he was reasonably sure I had not read; then, like a pedantic bibliographer, he would pronounce his opinion on some abstruse point. Such an academic divagation served him as a counteragent for keeping his strained physicochemical system in equilibrium. I much preferred this intellectuality of his to a flight into fantasy propelled by a narcotic. Sherlock Holmes was obviously deeply affected by the suicide of the revolutionist's daughter. He sat in his chair as if in mourning, silent, the fingers of his hands upraised and touching their tips in a triangle—almost like a ritual of prayer.

Mrs. Hudson's knock once more reminded us of the everyday world. "There are two gentlemen downstairs who wish to see you urgently, Mr. Holmes."

Holmes bade her show the two callers to our room. We heard mounting foot steps that climbed slowly, as if the climbers too were in mourning. Then the two men were before us; both were about or close to fifty years of age; both were simply dressed; one was unmistakably middle class, but the other a workingman. The first had a bearded, gentle countenance, with friendly shining eyes; the second had a grayish mustache and appeared somewhat distraught and even ill at ease. I vaguely recalled having seen his face before, but could not make my memory precise. The bearded one advanced towards us with a friendly handshake and said in excellent, though accented speech: "My name is Edward Bernstein, correspondent for German social-democratic newspapers, and this is my friend, Mr. Frederick Demuth.

Holmes responded in a kindly tone, as if in condolence: "Mr. Bernstein, I presume, the executor of our late friend Mr. Friedrich Engels and the author of that informative book *Ferdinand Lassalle as a Social Reformer,* translated by one now tragically dead by her own hand, Eleanor Marx Aveling."

Edward Bernstein shook his head in a dissenting negation: "No doubt," he said, "it was Tussy's own hand that administered the lethal draught, but the will that guided her hand was not her own but that of Edward Aveling."

Holmes was silent for a moment. "And you, Mr. Demuth," said Holmes, "were, I believe, the good friend of the unhappy Eleanor Marx Aveling."

Frederick Demuth nodded in agreement: "She was as fine a woman as ever walked the earth, Mr. Holmes; I am only a steam-fitter by trade, Mr. Holmes, with little book learning, but she would sit with me at our home, play with my little Harry, and talk to me about books, plays, and politics. She always seemed to hope that I would get interested in politics and become ambitious to be an officer in my union, the Amalgamated Society of Engineers. But I don't have much ambition in me and think the world a poor place, and if I needed any proof of that, it's the way a saint like Tussy was driven to death by a scamp like Aveling."

Holmes signified his assent: "I had occasion, Mr. Demuth, to learn sixteen years ago of the villainy of Dr. Edward Aveling. I have followed his career from year to year, noting the acts of evil that have been its trail. Mr. Bernard Shaw would occasionally inform me as to the activities of both Eleanor Marx and Edward Aveling. And I have kept up faithfully with the plays that Bernard Shaw has written by joining the London Stage Society and have

enjoyed watching him lecturing the actors. He once told me that
Eleanor Marx always hoped that her love would redeem her scoundrel husband. Aveling is a man of near genius, but with no sense of
honor, says Shaw. I think he is right. Eleanor Marx lived and died
hoping that her love could transform evil into good by some
philosophical chemistry; she knew as little of the laws and varieties
of human character as did her father.''

Edward Bernstein interjected with his low voice and gentle manner: ''I fear, Mr. Holmes, that our whole socialist movement is
vulnerable to such men of evil intent as Dr. Edward Aveling.
Before his death, Friedrich Engels and I argued about this for
several years. I said that unless the socialist movement adheres to
the highest principles and teaches the working class that man is an
end in himself, never to be used solely as a means, our movement
would degenerate into an organization of immoralists who would
stop at nothing to conquer power and who, having won it, would
use it ruthlessly to keep themselves in power, no matter how much
they would have to crush people's aspirations to freedom.''

''But certainly, Mr. Bernstein,'' responded Holmes, ''you must
have thought Karl Marx himself a man of the highest ethical aims,
devoted to what he thought was the emancipation of the working
class.''

''I only met Karl Marx in the last two years of his life,'' Bernstein answered, ''when August Bebel and I came to London in
November 1880 to visit Marx and Engels. None of us knew the
Marx of his stormy young revolutionary days. I have the feeling,
however, that there was not much difference between him and the
anarchists in those days. There was all the talk of 'seizing power'
and 'dictatorship of the proletariat' and 'smashing the state.' The
greatest good fortune for Marx was that he lived for more than
thirty years in England. He learned something about democracy,
parliaments, parties, elections, and he came to detest Bakunin and
the anarchists who organized themselves into secret societies and
plotted and praised terrorist actions while regarding themselves as
exempt from all moral law. Nevertheless, Marx never stopped calling me a Kantian sentimentalist; he said the working class could do
without 'ideological nonsense,' as he called it, about rights, duty,
and liberty. I could never accept Marx's saying that the socialist

movement was based on no ethical principle but completely on the inevitable decline of capitalism. How does one decide on whether to cooperate with the inevitable or resist and postpone it? And maybe what we choose and decide of our own free will partially determines what will happen. I wish you and I could discuss these questions over a plate of frankfurters and a bottle of beer, Mr. Holmes, but Mr. Demuth and I have come to consult you about the sad death of Eleanor Marx.''

''Pray,'' said Holmes thoughtfully, ''please do not hesitate to ask my advice or services in any way that I can be of help, Mr. Bernstein and Mr. Demuth.''

The workingman now began to speak: ''I wish I knew more of philosophy, and history, and political economy, Mr. Holmes, but I am just a toolmaker and machinist. I can't say I'm a socialist; I'm just a member of my union, which tries to get us the best wages and conditions it can, but I'm not sure that socialist bosses would be any better than the company's kind; in fact, from what I've seen of the socialists, I think they'd be a lot worse. Mind you, I don't include Eleanor among them, because she was a saint, and it was a socialist and his socialist twaddle that led her down the way to drinking poison. And I don't have any respect for these men, Marx and Engels. At the trade union headquarters, Will Thorne and Hyndman have placed pictures of the old men to hang on our walls. But from what my old mother told me before she died, as far as I am concerned they were both fit for another kind of hanging. I might as well tell you, Mr. Holmes, my mother was the servant to the Marx family all her life. She adored Mrs. Marx and the children. But Karl Marx used her to practice the free-love theories in which he believed in those days. I am Marx's own son, though he never acknowledged me or set his eyes on me. Engels took me in hand jovially and put me out to live with nursing-women's families in Manchester and London. My mother used to visit me on holidays. Once when her mistress was unhappy and half-demented with her master's refusal to get a job to earn the bread for his family, she told me of this man so learned in books and so indifferent to the human heart.''

Holmes listened thoughtfully. There was a simple humanity about Holmes that drew forth the confidences of men and women alike. Here, they felt, was a man who for all his calmness and analytic power sympathized with their plight and would put all his powers and intelligence at their service.

Frederick Demuth continued: "What blasted Tussy's life is that she learned the truth of her father's personal life. But she loved him all the more, because she knew the terrible misery of their household. And she was determined to prove to herself and the world that she could be as self-denying as her mother had been. I had no father to guide my life. Tussy had both a father and mother. One was a domineering man who demanded sacrifices from others to make his life easy; the other was a submissive woman who had decided to sacrifice herself. So the daughter lived out the play again in her own life, giving herself for Edward Aveling and something she called 'class struggle.' But I think she realized at the end that it had all been for nothing, and she killed herself."

An anger issued from this workingman that was so intense in its flux that, if Edward Aveling had chanced to enter our rooms, Demuth would have swept him away, I felt, entirely.

At this point, however, Bernstein interposed, with his pleading, persuasive rationality: "Surely, Fred," he said, "Tussy's work will always be remembered by us and the movement and be appreciated. She was more than just the mistress of an unworthy man. She wrote useful, helpful articles for our movement; she translated great literature and extended the community that binds all men of good will; she gave many workingmen the sense that they were more than just hands to move machines, that there was something godlike in every man."

Fred Demuth drew from his coat-pocket several letters. "Let me read to you, Mr. Holmes, from Tussy's last letters to me, and let me ask you whether there is any way that we could put Edward Aveling in the dock and try him for contributing to the death of Eleanor Marx."

I can now remember only parts of what Frederick Demuth read. I recall his low, tense voice reading from three letters that had been written in February and March 1898. His voice would falter with emotion, and once even broke for several seconds, as he endeavored to regain his equanimity. Eleanor Marx wrote of how much she owed to the friendship of her rejected half-brother, how he was "one of the greatest and best men" she had known. She thought that in his natural kindness he would never understand such a morally sick person as Edward Aveling. Some people, she wrote, simply lack a "moral sense," just as others are deficient in their sense of hearing or sight. She felt she had to help cure such a person, but in doing so she had undergone "long suffering," whose details were so shocking that she could not tell them even to Fred Demuth. But her suffering had brought her understanding; a French proverb said, "To understand is to forgive." She, however, had no need even to forgive, because she could only love. Her last letter, written soon before her self-inflicted death, told of the "little hope" that was left to her; what was there to live for? "Why we all go on like this I do not understand." She was "ready to go" and would do so "with joy," but so long as Aveling needed her she felt she was bound to remain.

Demuth could scarce bring himself to read this last sentence. I reflected that this woman, his half-sister, friend of the literary lights of her generation, the educated child of the most illustrious of the revolutionary "intellectuals" (as they now call them) finally found herself adrift in a spiritual void; the ideological formulae upon which she had been nurtured seemed equations with meaningless solutions. Was Edward Aveling's cynicism toward human ethics essentially any different from the creed of her own father and his friend Engels? Hadn't they too mocked at the "moral sense" as a bourgeois invention? Fred Demuth muttered bitterly that none of the communist philosophers had any moral sense. Tussy, he said, had once looked through the letters of her father and Engels. She found several that referred mockingly to himself, Fred Demuth, as their second *Communist Manifesto,* a second instance of their collaboration; Marx did the siring, while Engels took responsibility for the upbringing.

"I have heard much talk of 'bourgeois hypocrisy,' Mr. Holmes, but it's a mite compared to the socialist kind. But I come back to my question: Is there any way, Mr. Holmes, that we can bring Edward Aveling to justice? His signature got her the poison from the chemist's. He used to preach at her that, if love were gone from one's life and one's capacity to serve the revolutionary cause had faded, then the time had come to take one's life. He used to tell her there was both a right and a duty to commit suicide and would recite her lots of examples from savage tribes, Romans, Hindus, and Eskimos. What is more, the inspector at Scotland Yard told me that Aveling destroyed the last letter that Tussy had received the morning of the day she died."

Holmes looked alert. "Do you have any idea, Mr. Demuth, from whom that letter was?"

"That's exactly what Inspector Lestrade asked me. I told him the letter was from me."

Holmes regarded Frederick Demuth closely. "Might I then presume to inquire as to what you had written to Eleanor Marx? It is indeed important that I know," Holmes said with emphasis.

Demuth for a moment looked desperate with anger at what he was going to say. "Tussy," he said, "received a message about two weeks ago that Edward Aveling under his stage name 'Alec Nelson' had married a young actress in theatricals, a Miss Eva Frye. This Miss Frye is a bold one. She asked Tussy to send her money to care for Edward on the nights he spent with her. Tussy couldn't believe Edward Aveling would sink to this lowest villainy. She thought that, since the first Mrs. Aveling had died a year ago, she would be the second if there ever was any. She asked me to see this Eva Frye. It took me a few days to locate her, and she was saucy and impertinent when I saw her in her flat. But she showed me the marriage certificate and gave me the details. As plain as anything, Dr. Aveling and she were wed. She told me a few more things that I shall never mention. Tussy had asked me to let her know by mail what I found out. I did so and urged her at the same time to leave this worthless Aveling to his newly found companion and rebuild her own life. She had many friends who loved her, I reminded her. But life was now drained of its meaning for her. Aveling is probably waiting to inherit her estate."

We all sat quietly as Frederick Demuth concluded his recital of the last events in the life of Eleanor Marx. In death she had liberated herself from degradation and deception; yet her life's sacrifice had been a mistake from beginning to end.

Edward Bernstein with his simple, straightforward sense returned us to the world of sanity. "As I see it, Mr. Holmes, our problem is whether we can ask for Aveling's indictment on some clear charge, and assuming that we succeed in so doing, whether we can prosecute him while preventing him at the same time from revealing the facts of Marx's fatherhood of Mr. Demuth?''

Holmes nodded his approval: ''You put it most clearly, Mr. Bernstein. Aveling would surely try to establish a long previous history of Eleanor Marx's depressions and would argue that her own father's conduct was in large part their cause. I doubt whether a British court would exclude such evidence as irrelevant. And, since Edward Aveling was actually at the Social Democratic Federation headquarters when Eleanor Marx swallowed the poison, it would be most difficult to establish that he was an effective causal agent in her act. The jury might be inclined to find it at least reasonably possible that the poison, if Aveling had signed the order, was meant to eliminate some old dog; in any case, Aveling might argue that he had found by experience that Eleanor Marx's hysterias were best counteracted by bringing her face-to-face with the reality of self-destruction. Many a threat of suicide dissolves when the chance of its accomplishment is made available. We can be sure that the reputation of the Marx family would emerge much tarnished, while Edward Aveling would present himself as the long-suffering protector of a hysterical woman; his secret marriage to a young actress he would explain as an act done in desperation with Eleanor's persistent irrationality, and never intended seriously, since he had used another name. It would be a most unpleasant case. The jury might find Edward Aveling a most reprehensible character. It is doubtful, however, that they would find him guilty, in a legal sense, of any crime.''

The workingman Demuth replied as if in bitter surrender: ''Then Edward Aveling can blackmail us and Tussy's memory and the whole international socialist movement by threatening to reveal publicly that I am Karl Marx's illegitimate son. No wonder the London socialists want me to hide my face, and look embarrassed when they meet me. Abraham sent Ishmael into the desert to die, and Marx and his disciples would have wanted Freddie Demuth to vanish in London's slums.''

Holmes was plainly respectful of the honest bitterness of the workingman. He tried to comfort him. ''Your mother must have been a remarkable woman, Mr. Demuth, always patient, always loyal.''

"Yes, Mr. Holmes, that she was. When she would come to visit me, she would sit quietly, and when I railed at things, she would say that was the way the world was. Once I asked her, 'Mother, what do you think of all this socialism that your master Marx preached?' She shrugged her shoulders and said: 'The master was a dreamer. He would never look for a job even while we were starving. I would go out and work for others for a day or half-day and come back with a shilling to buy potatoes. But Mrs. Marx was a loving soul; I used to wish she had listened to her older brother, who became Bismarck's minister, when he warned her against throwing away her life on this spoiled Jewish bookworm. He never should have said 'Jewish,' because that made Jenny so indignant that she was more determined than ever to marry her Karl. As for myself, I always worshiped my God and did my duty, and paid no attention when our master talked as if he knew more than God. The world isn't going to change. People now ride railways and light gas-fires, whereas we used to walk and kindled candles; but we are all as miserable as we ever were.'

"I asked her whether she didn't feel angry at what her master had done to her. She answered that the same happened to most servant girls and that she at least had not been turned out of the house. When I replied sarcastically that the Marx family couldn't do that because she was taking care of all of them for nothing, she began to cry. We would put our arms around each other."

We listened wordlessly; what could Holmes or I respond to this unadorned, heartfelt eloquence? Holmes stoked the flickering fire, and said reflectively: "Perhaps a punishment awaits Edward Aveling sooner than he expects. Yesterday I met Sir Edwin Ray Lankester and his friend, Dr. Horace Donkin, at the St. Bartholomew Hospital. They told me that Edward Aveling's illness would end his life before the year was over."

Our visitors rose. Bernstein shook our hands warmly, saying he hoped soon to send us a copy of his forthcoming book criticizing the foundations of Marx's socialist ideology; he wished very much to have Holmes's opinion. Again, he thanked us in memory of Tussy. Mr. Frederick Demuth bowed and thanked Holmes for his courtesy and good advice.

We observed the ever-changing shapes of our fireplace flames in silence. Holmes was lost in reverie.

"In years to come, Watson, our society may have to pay terribly for the loss of its moral rudder, even as Eleanor Marx learned through bitter events that her father had maimed the moral sense. Last week at the Athenaeum Club I heard old Herbert Spencer remark that we live in an era of rebarbarization. One sign of it is that the moral sense is so disparaged by our advanced thinkers; thus we will retrogress from civilization to barbarism."

"Do you mean to say, Holmes, that Karl Marx was an agent of rebarbarization?"

"Marx thought he stood for progress. He was powerfully righteous in condemning the capitalist system, but he never explored closely what would be the consequences of the system he advocated. I don't think he wanted to know. He avoided reading what John Stuart Mill and Herbert Spencer wrote about bureaucratic compression and the liberty-hating drive of socialist planners. Spencer warned that socialist societies had an affinity for militarism. He once wanted to meet Marx and raise his objections. But Marx begged off with some hollow remarks about Spencer piling up facts the way a shopkeeper arranges his merchandise. Actually I think Marx was scared. Lankester tells me he always avoided meeting real scientists; he preferred to be surrounded by a circle of uneducated admirers, a shaman for the rebarbarizers. We must go see Bernard Shaw's new play *Candida*. I hear it has a Fabian socialist hero. Shaw will entertain England into socialism, but I don't think he really knows where he's taking us anymore than Marx did. Probably he'll now make a comedy out of Eleanor Marx's suicide."

Finally I might add, Irene Adler remained ever-present in Holmes's thoughts and activites. Every few months he would receive a charming and delightful letter from her. She described her classes in singing at the East Side Settlement House that she had founded. She told how her young boys almost worshiped her when they discovered that she was a personal friend of the great Sherlock Holmes; how the volumes of my stories about him in the settlement library were dog-eared, weather-beaten, and hand-worn; how the rumor circulated in little socialist meeting-halls that the great Karl Marx himself had invoked the aid of Sherlock Holmes. Holmes for a few days after each of her letters seemed to live in the highest sphere.

Indeed, I may now divulge that in response to her urgings Holmes journeyed several times to the United States. It was her plea that had led to his undertaking in 1893 on behalf of the governor of Illinois, John P. Altgeld, a highly confidential study. Holmes examined minutely the evidence submitted during the trial of the anarchists charged with perpetrating the Haymarket bombing outrages in 1886. His study persuaded the governor that the three anarchists, still alive and imprisoned, deserved pardon.

Sherlock Holmes, indeed, after his work on behalf of Marx in the case of the old revolutionist's daughter, was consulted quite frequently by revolutionists in all sorts of predicaments. They knew he had no sympathy with either their political aims or their methods, but they valued highly what they oddly called his "dialectics." Holmes could never manage to get them to explain to him what they meant by that word. One of them especially used it, a Mr. Vladimir Ulyanov, who became well known in later years under the sobriquet of "V. I. Lenin." He came to consult Holmes in 1908 at a time when the Russian socialists were holding a conclave in London. He was much disturbed by rumors that one of his henchmen, a certain Joseph Stalin, had met with remnants of Professor Moriarty's old gang; the purported aim of this coalition was to carry out an "expropriation" of some British "bourgeois" bank in order to pay for the conclave's expenses and subsidize further revolutionary agitation. Mr. Ulyanov wished to know more about the Moriarty gang; I gathered he was less concerned with the morality of expropriation than with the anarchist-Bakuninist affiliation of the Moriarty gang. I am not yet at liberty to narrate the details of that delicate case or to tell how a naif American millionaire was persuaded to finance Mr. Ulyanov's activities.